# REBOUND

## THE GANG

--- PULLING THREADS ---

Book Fifteen

SHERYLL O'BRIEN

This is a work of fiction. All characters in this book are the product of an overactive imagination. Any businesses, organizations, places, events, and incidents are used fictionally. Any resemblance to a real person, living or dead, is a tremendous coincidence.

ISBN 978-1-939351-38-8

Printed in United States of America

Mom,

On July 1, 2021,
Rebound will be published.


It marks the end of the series—
Not the end of the story.

I promise.

# ACKNOWLEDGMENT

As we end the Pulling Threads series, I would like to thank the readers who have come along for the journey, and tell my wonderful character friends that I love them and I will miss them.

A particular shout out to the women of Pulling Threads. You fill the pages with grace, you conquer self-doubts, you champion for truth and justice, you push into conflict when you just want to breathe, you outwit your opponents, overcome their abuses, offer words of wisdom, and wreak havoc on those in your way—and you enjoy the hell out of your men—those sexy as hell men of Pulling Threads. So to Kit, Joy, Maura, Annie, Leavy, Sage, Gretchen, Peyton, Mama Girl, Faye, Stacy, Dominique, Celia, Shelby, and Felicity, thanks for the laughs and love.

A heartfelt thank you to my team:

Andria Flores ~ Editor extraordinaire.
Nancy Pendleton ~ Goddess of the publishing world.
Jessica Champion ~ Web designer and manager.
25 Hours Consulting
Daryl Bruinsma ~ Cover Design & Animation.


A special thank you:

To my wonderful friend, Donna Eaton, who has read every word of everything I have ever written—when she could have been reading her favorites: Sandford and Patterson. Thank you for taking the journey with me. Muah!

# Testimonials

"One book will set the hook!" ~ Nancy Pendleton

"This avid reader predicts that Sheryll O'Brien will become your favorite author. She's mine." ~ Ruth S. Bodreau

"The characters draw you in immediately. You will worry, laugh, hope, and love right along with them." ~ Donna Eaton

"There is nothing sweeter than a Sunday morning coffee, a blanket, overcast skies, and a *Pulling Threads* novel." ~ Andria Flores

"Everything you'd want in a good book. Humor, romance, suspense and great characters! It even takes place by the ocean! Loved it." ~ Helena Green

"I could write a book about the wonderfulness of it all." ~ Faith

"Hunks, humor, and heartache! What more could you ask for?" ~ Marjorie McCarthy

"*Bullet Bungalow* is a page turning family saga and then *Netti Barn* and *Cutters Cove* come along and add a whole lot of trauma to the drama." ~ Jessica O'Brien

"The most promising new author I've encountered in my publishing career!" ~ Jim P. – Woodwind Press

# --- Pulling Threads ---

Bullet Bungalow
Netti Barn
Cutters Cove
They Run
They Hide
They Choose

### PENOBSCOT BAY
#### A Rocco Fiancetti Incorporated Investigation

Reasons
Rescues
Resolutions
Torment
Tango
Tests
Resolve
Revenge
Rebound

Coming someday…
Alva


# ~~~ Twisted Threads ~~~

Her Scream

Coming soon…

Stay Safe
Ashore on Stony Beach

*End line.*


      Malcolm Price is in the grips of a nightmare. He's the lone Spur banging the boards at the AT&T Center in San Antonio, Texas. It's a championship game and there are no black and silvers on the court with him. There's no offense, no defense—just him. The point guard scans for his team as he toes for a jump ball. He abandons the search and runs his own game. The One locks himself in the key, fighting invisible opponents for shots and rebounds. He hears breathing and the squeak of sneakers on the parquet. He feels the bang and push of bodies hard against him. But he cannot find anyone. "Where?" The sound of his pounding heart is deafening. Sweat runs his face and stings his eyes. He swipes his arm across his forehead, runs his hands across his chest, his team jersey no longer there to dry them. He checks the scoreboard, the Spurs are losing by 2020 points, he is losing by 2020 points. He checks the stands for the man who can help him win. He wants that man to play the game with him. He fears he'll lose if he plays alone. "Where?" The player known worldwide as 77 benches himself, dries his sweat, catches his breath, and does a frantic search of the arena again. He finds the man he needs sitting in the stands. **"Help me,"** he cries out.

The man stands and turns to leave, "You don't need my help, son. You can win on your own."

The battered man wakes from
that nightmare—
to find he's in the grips of another.


From this nightmare, Malcolm Price
will never wake.

# Rebound

*Off the grid.*

## Layne

The assassin of Senator Curtis Morgan has been on the road since January 20th. She was heading back to Blue Marsh Lake, Pennsylvania, after the shooting in Skidaway, Georgia, when she was warned away...

"RFI is hunting you hard, Layne. You've got money and fake IDs, ditch the F-150, get a new ride and go dark. Stay away from anyone associated with The Realm, don't go anywhere near Eli Reynolds, and don't come back to High Noone. If you do, I'll take you out, myself."

She pulls a breath, tiring from the simple effort. Her exhaustion is heavy upon her, she swipes at a falling tear, "Don't blame you, Sarge, but I sure could use a place to rest up, and for more than one damn night at a time." She takes a look in the rearview before exiting the highway and slows to a near crawl as she travels the ramp. "Let's see who follows me off the interstate." She scans the vehicles as they ready to pull into traffic. "Family of four. Couple of high school sweethearts. Trucker. No tail." She hangs a right onto a two-lane and follows signs to a strip of fast food joints, "Damn, this is the muthaload. Burgers with and without special sauces, fried chicken, pizza, tacos, soups, salads, and restrooms. I need to piss, then I need to eat."

She parks near a trendy restaurant, heads inside, places an order for a "Pick Two: bowl of cheddar broccoli and chicken salad sandwich with a large, iced tea to go." She uses the restroom, grabs her food, and starts for the F-150. Changing her mind midway, she takes a seat at an outdoor café table, "Cold, but sunny." Layne eagerly chomps at her sandwich while the soup cools, she keeps her eyes fixed on the parking lot entrance. She might have seen Fred Serpico pull in if she hadn't been distracted by a big-ass rider on a big-ass Harley who circled the lot and parked 100 feet from her table. She waits through the kick-standing, dismounting, unhelmeting, and back stretching before following Harley Man inside.

Layne steps in line behind the MAN who's wearing the hell out of a pair of well-worn jeans, black leather jacket, and biker boots. She smiles when she sees the eagle talon tattoos on each knuckle. "Nice ride."

He smiles wide, takes a long, **hard** look at the raven-haired, golden-eyed, bronze-skinned, banging hot babe, "You referring to me or my bike, darlin?"

"Both." She nods her head in the direction of the counter, "You're up."

He adjusts his wood, "Sure am," he smiles wide. "I'll order after you."

"Large black coffee and a chocolate-chip cookie," she shrugs a shoulder and flips her hair from it.

He laughs big, "Make it two, and make them to go."

"Are we going somewhere?"

"You up for a ride?"

"On you or your bike?"

"Both."

"Don't want to leave my truck in the lot, so how about I follow you out."

He pays for their coffees and cookies and lets her pass, "After you darlin."

She smiles wide, "Hope that's your game plan between the sheets."

"Damn straight, Woman. Name's Gunner in case it matters."

"It doesn't."


Fred


The RFI detective watches from across the crowded parking lot as Harley Man walks Assassin Babe to her truck, hands off a tray with two coffees and a brown paper sack, gets on his bike, and leads the way out. "Looks like Hungry Hitwoman chose more than a Pick Two." Fred watches GPS for a few minutes, "Good, they're staying on local roads." He hits a burger joint, a pizza parlor, and a taco stand for a shitload of artery-clogging cuisine, packs his jaw full of pepperoni pizza, then pulls from his parking space. "Gonna be a long night, or maybe a few long days if Harley Man enjoys his ride."

Fred lets the biker lead the babe to the hookup hideaway, pulls into a high school parking lot to give the twosome time to settle, then sets out to find them. The steady red on his GPS tracker shows Layne's truck is stopped and hasn't moved in 30 minutes. He follows several residential streets off the two-lane to a gravel road cut through a wooded area. He stops when he comes to a big-ass sign that reads, **Private Property – Stay Out Muthafucker**. "No problem, Harley Man."

Fred web-maps the area looking for a place to park his ride and grab some shuteye, "Few motels, but kinda far from lover's lane. This is gonna be tricky. Upside—she hasn't figured her truck is trapped, and she'll stay put for a while. Downside—she knows about the trap and drops it at Harley Man's place, in which case I won't know, maybe for days, that she's gone." He scans his surroundings, "I need to move. Can't risk being called in for a 'strange car' complaint, so it looks like I'm heading back to the high school for a stretch." He parks in an upper lot that's plenty full, stuffs his face with takeout, and silently reviews his log.

January 20: Pittsburg, PA.
January 21: Morgantown, WV.
January 22: Charleston, WV.
January 23: Columbus, OH.
January 24: Pittsburg, PA.
January 25: Parkersburg, WV.
January 26: Morgantown, WV.
January 27-28: Pittsburg, PA.

"Okay, it's January 29th, and we're near Morgantown again. We're still looping because she's reeling from the hit. Reality is setting in. She can't go home or to any ranger friends, she probably wants to go to El for help, but so far she's resisted the pull. Please go to Eli."

He finishes his second taco, pushes his seat w.a.y. back and plans things out. "I'll give you a few more days to think this shit through, but if you don't head toward Alaska soon, I'm taking you in, Layne Osterman." Fred cranks Bob Seger's, *Roll Me Away*, and starts thinking about the woman who sent him away…

Fred watched Kitt loop the track at the Athletic Center for a couple minutes before entering. He took a seat on a bleacher, put his elbows onto the bench behind him, and stretched his long legs out in front. He tried to make eye contact with Kitt when she rounded the far end of the quarter mile track. She averted his stare, her facial expression tightened, and her body pushed its limits. She passed by without so much as a look his way. On her fourth loop, he got off his duff and jogged diagonally across the track, arriving seconds before she rounded the far corner. She made a move to round him. He cut her off.

"Move," pant, pant, pant, "Fred."

She bobbed.

He weaved.

"Kittridge, stop." He took hold of her wrist. "Stop."

"Why are you," pant, pant, pant, "here?"

"Why are you punishing yourself?"

She shook off his hand, "Steve shouldn't have called you."

"Yeah, well he did."

"He should mind his business."

"Yeah? And me?"

"You should mind your business, too." She swiped at sweat along her brow and stepped around him.

He let her. When he got to the exit, he called over his shoulder, "You're pregnant, Kittridge."

She stopped running at the sound of the slamming door.

~

"Detective Serpico, this is Agent Hayes. Kitt is with me at the lower level medical unit. She's had an emotional response to today's event and is currently resting here. I think you might…"

"Where is she?" Fred asked from the doorway.

Candace laughed, "That was fast. She's resting in there—you can go in, but do not disturb her. Got it?"

"Got it." Fred moved quietly into the exam room, leaned against a wall, and took in the beauty of Kittridge Anne Mahoney. He exhaled the breath he'd been holding for hours and banged their recent conversation through his head. He stopped when he got to the question she asked, the one he never answered. "I'm here because I love you."

Kitt stirred. "I know you love me, Fred, but I need you to leave. This is something I need to do on my own."

He pushed off the wall and took a seat on the edge of her bed, "Your way through something—or away from something?"

"I don't know."

He took her hand. She threaded their fingers together. "You need to leave."

He kissed her hand. He walked away.

Kittridge Mahoney and Fred Serpico are taking some time to work through some shit— the thing is, they aren't working the same shit— and they are thousands of miles away from one another…

"Hey, Kittridge."

"Fred. I'm sorry about Senator Morgan."

"Yeah."

"Do you need to talk?"

"About us." **Fred heard her sigh, he pushed in.** "Are things still bad between us?"

"Where are you, Fred? The team thinks you're trailing Layne Osterman."

"The team's right. Don't tell them I called. I don't want interference—this is something I need to do on my own."

"Sounds reasonable when you say it."

**He felt the sting of her affront.** "So things are still bad between us."

"Not between us, Fred. Things are bad for me."

"Then things are bad for us, Kittridge. I've been thinking about Roni lately."

"Well, that's good to hear."

**He laughed,** "Kittridge, you asked me once why I wasn't with my ex-wife anymore. Do you remember what I said?"

"That her undercover work and the constant worry about her became too much."

"And that I gave Roni an ultimatum: me or the job."

"I remember. Is there a point to this walk down memory lane?"

"Kittridge, I understand how hard it is to be the one waiting and not knowing. How impossible it is to separate from the fear of losing someone long enough to pull some air. What I want you to understand is this—if fear won't let you breathe, we leave RFI. We go back to Bullet Bungalow or to the moon, that's what we do. Kittridge, I will always choose you, choose us." **Fred heard her sigh, and he pulled back.**

"I need to go. Please stay safe, Fred."

"Give our boy a kiss and our baby bump a little rub for me." **He waited for something more. She hung up.**

**Every night since January 20, Fred's called home. Some nights he filled the silence— most nights he listened to his woman's struggle to fill an emotional hole caused by a bullet—the one that tore through him nearly a year ago.**

# Funeral Service
# Curtis Robert Morgan

Senator Morgan, from the great state of Georgia, was assassinated twelve days ago. Within minutes of his death pronouncement, the wheels of politics rolled over his carcass and steered toward his heir apparent. Calls raised swiftly for Malcolm Price to step in line as a 2020 presidential candidate for the Democratic Party. He turned a deaf ear to those calls. Political pundits went 24/7 dissecting Marist, PPP, Quinnipiac, Pew, Siena, and Ipsos polls—all confirming Malcolm Price as an ideal candidate for a presidential run. He turned a blind eye to the numbers. When reporters surrounded his home in Lewisburg, he escaped to Skidaway Island and locked himself behind the closed doors of his father's study where he grieved privately, railed mightily, prayed openly, and wrote, and wrote, and wrote. And when he had rubbed his heart and soul plenty raw, he had a eulogy worthy of the senator, of his father. Malcolm Price plans to deliver the Skidaway Speech, as it has come to be known by the women in his life—but you know what they say about best laid plans.

The Cathedral of Saint Peter and Saint Paul, located in the northwest part of Washington, DC, at Wisconsin and Massachusetts Avenues, is known worldwide as Washington National Cathedral. It is a stately, religious, and historic edifice. The cornerstone of the Neo-gothic structure was laid in 1907 in the presence of President Theodore Roosevelt. Its final finial was placed 83 years later during a ceremony attended by President George H. W. Bush. For decades, the Cathedral has hosted funerals and memorial services for American presidents and other notable public servants and celebrated figures. Today, the Cathedral is wall to wall with political movers and shakers. Some have come to honor a senior statesman. Others have come to rub elbows with the politically powerful. All have come to witness a son eulogize a father he's known a handful of months.

Malcolm Price stands from his seat in the front row and places a kiss on the clasped hand of his wife. The bereaved man straightens himself then steps from a place of personal reflection to a place of public scrutiny. The imposing 6'5" figure ignores the flag-draped casket as he passes by. If he stops to touch it, he won't be able to settle his emotions, and he won't be able to speak about his loss, the country's loss. He takes a minute at the lectern, scans the Cathedral for familiar faces amongst the shoulder to shoulder congregants. He receives nods from former Presidents George W. Bush and Barack Obama, and warm smiles from First Ladies, Laura Bush and Michelle Obama. Though these men and women served their country from different sides of the aisle, today they unite to honor a senator who helped bridge the gap of political dogma—a man both presidents thought of as a friend.

Malcolm Price pulls a deep breath, opens a folder that'd been placed at the podium, and removes his prepared speech from within. He silently reads the first few words before replacing it and closing the cover. "I prepared something for today's service, but my written words do not express the important things. They do not convey how unprepared I am to face the great and small things ahead without my father—and yet, here I am facing the greatest challenge of my life." Malcolm stops to allow the crack of emotion pass then begins again, "My father left this world violently, unnecessarily, and far too soon for his family, not only those assembled here today, but those across this great Nation. Senator Morgan thought of every American as a family member. He toiled on their behalf and prayed that his efforts made their lives better." The grieving son pulls a steadying breath before heading down a whole new path.

"We are not in this house of worship because Heaven beckoned my father. Curtis

Robert Morgan was thrust from his earthly home. I believe my father sits in the presence of his Heavenly father, but he is there because certain people rejected the call of higher angels, because certain factions answered the clang of demonic forces. Those whose ambitions are self-serving, whose intentions are held in secret, whose sinister selves lurk and plan in dark corners determined the fate of Curtis Morgan." His eyes travel from person to person, lock onto those who squirm a bit too much and a bit too long. He ends his visual claim at his father's casket. "Senator Morgan harbored no sinister thoughts. He shared his vision for this country openly. He did not cloak his ambitions in secrecy or tend to them in darkness; he told the world who he was and what he stood for every day through words and deeds. My father is no longer able to work for the people of this country. He is no longer able to speak on their behalf, so I will speak for him. I implore you to look at the people in this beautiful house of worship—really look. There are two groups in attendance today, those who celebrate the goodness of Curtis Robert Morgan and those who feared it. The latter of the two should continue to fear it."

Malcolm takes a moment and shoulders the weight of the room ... of his calling. He tries to calm the shake of his hand with a gentle tap of the leather-bound folder. He lifts his head and accepts his role. "I am the son of Curtis Robert

Morgan; I was to be his vice-presidential running mate." Malcolm looks to the three women in the front pew and awaits their silent approval. One by one, they nod. He looks out over those who eagerly crave his next words and those who dread them. He catches a subtle movement and looks once again toward the former presidents, receiving a nod from Mr. Bush and the beginning of Mr. Obama's ubiquitous, broad smile.

The Man of the Moment descends the altar stairs, stands perfectly still, clearly in deep thought. He places his gigantic hand onto the flag-draped casket, pulls the last measure of energy between the two men, and makes the last moments they will ever share the most profound. "On the fifth day of November in the year 2019, Curtis Robert Morgan declared his candidacy for president of the United States. Today, I follow in my father's footsteps and echo his intentions. I would be honored to serve the people of this great Nation as President of the United States if they will have me. I officially declare as an Independent candidate and humbly request the people's vote on the third day of November in the year 2020."

*Sit the fuck down.*

Members of the disbanded Gang of Eight were dispersed throughout the Cathedral when Malcolm Price threw his political hat into the ring. One by one, they excused themselves, inched their way along packed pews, and headed toward the nearest exit. One by one, they left messages on Felicity Ferraro's voicemail—all demanding a meeting, two of them threatening bodily harm if their next call wasn't answered. She takes none of their calls, but turns on the television hoping something will shed light on the barrage of incoming voicemails.

**Breaking news: Malcolm Price, son of slain Georgia Senator, Curtis Morgan, announced his candidacy for President of the United States at the funeral service for his father. The newly elected mayor of Lewisburg, Pennsylvania, has abandoned the Democratic Party and will be running for president as an Independent. His most likely opponents in the general election are Democratic Senator, Jim Morrisey out of the state of Missouri, who saw a bump in his polling after the death of Curtis Morgan and Republican Senator, Turner Rodgers, out of the state of Pennsylvania, who has been leading in the GOP polls since announcing his candidacy.**

"Well, that explains the phone calls. I suspect I'll be hearing from Mr. Reynolds about this." She turns off the T.V. and remains in the den. She eyes her surroundings yet again. "Not sure which rooms in my home have eyes and ears in them, but I'm hoping this isn't one of them." She goes to the wet bar, opens a bottle of Pinot, pours herself a glass, and perches on the couch. A few glasses in, she succumbs to memories of her last conversation with The Body…

"Mrs. Ferraro, are you on the line?"

"Yes."

"The Realm is disbanded. You are the only one at the leadership level who is not free to move on."

The silence from Felicity's end was deafening.

"Are you still there, Mrs. Ferraro?"

"Yes."

"Good. This will be our final conversation, so please listen carefully. The obstacle between Turner Rodgers and his place in the White House is dead and will soon be buried. That ensures Turner's silence about the organization, its members, and its leader. If Turner is seated in the Oval Office a year from now, Roland Gaffney gets a pardon, which in turn ensures his silence. If by chance Rodgers loses his bid for president, both men will be dead within hours. As for the others, Eli will remain in hiding. An iron-clad file is being built to establish him as The Body of The Realm. Without Turner Rodgers and Roland Gaffney to dispute the evidence against Eli, my brother will assume all responsibilities for the organization. Upon learning of the disbandment, the Gang of Eight will be out for blood . They will not go after Turner—they will, however, bleed you dry. That should be payback enough for you Mrs. Ferraro, but there is more. We will get to that later. Are you still with me?"

"Yes."

"RFI and the FBI will continue to hunt me, regardless of what happens with my brother. They know I am The Body, but after Turner and Roland are handled, there will be no one alive to help them prove their case—except for you. My adversaries had better not learn anything from you. Is that clear?"

"Yes."

"Is that understood, Mrs. Ferraro?"

"Yes."

"Good. Think back to the last time we were together, and we were having a tense conversation and you were trying to get a rise out of me. I warned you against trying my patience. You tried it anyway. During that exchange you had a rather pithy question. Do you remember this event, Mrs. Ferraro?"

"Yes."

"Then you should remember your questioning words, but let me repeat them for you, **Or what, Mathis, you'll hit me? No, you don't hit women. Or maybe you'll kill me? Please do, it will put me out of my misery, so that's a win for me, really. If neither of those suffice, tell me, Mathis, what will you do if I try your patience?**"

There is deathly silence on Felicity's end.

Mathis breaks the silence. "I will do this."

He ended the call.

In a matter of seconds, she received a video text. It broke her heart.

Felicity is pulled from her stupor by his incoming call.

"You have a problem, Mrs. Ferraro. As you are aware, Malcolm Price declared his candidacy for president. The man has legions of loyal fans, and the enviable commodity of being well-liked and respected. More to the point, he has momentum. Before he even left the Cathedral, Price had garnered full-throated support of heavy-hitters in the Democratic party, despite his declaring as an Independent. If Price remains in the race, Turner Rodgers will not prevail. Your phone is blowing up because Gang members were at the funeral. They've put two and two together and know the consolation prizes Turner doled out last night will never come to pass. The Gang will not be getting cabinet posts and administrative positions, not if the 2020 election is a toe-to-toe between Rodgers and Price. During the past 24 hours, the Gang found themselves on their asses with no powerbase in The Realm or in DC. They're pretty pissed, Mrs. Ferraro. Are you still there?"

"Yes."

"Good. The Gang has called for a meeting with you and Rodgers. Return their calls and take the meeting. Tonight. They've had time to lick their wounds from the bomb you and Turner dropped last night. They didn't retaliate then for two reasons: they owned their stupidity for not knowing Turner wasn't The Body, and they settled for the crumbs Turner tossed at their feet. Today's event will cause some to seek immediate retribution. Now that Turner's future is in question, they will cut him off at the knees. Before they do that, they are going to want to know the identity of The Body. Like I said, Mrs. Ferraro, you have a problem. I expect you to fix it."

Felicity starts to say something, but stops when she realizes she's talking to dead air. She paces a circuitous route through her cavernous home banging the previous night's meeting through her head...

The energy in the room charged upward when Felicity Ferraro arrived with Turner Rodgers. Members of the Gang started talking over one another. Former Homeland Security Secretary, Carter Thorndyke, bellowed above the rest and moved threateningly toward the arrivals, "You'd better update us, Turner. My ass is going to be at the Cathedral tomorrow, and I demand to know if The Realm is responsible for Morgan's assassination. He's been dead nearly two fucking weeks, and none of us know a fucking thing."

"Step the fuck back, Carter ....... Now!" Rodgers demanded.

Thorndyke backed away.

"Sit down, all of you."

Felicity remained at Turner's side, though she wanted to take a seat,  needed to take a seat.

"This is the last time this group will be in the same room together, so pay attention. Over the course of the past few days, the organization has gone dark. This meeting marks the end of The Realm."

"The fuck it does."

"Sit down and shut up, Carter."

He refused to sit . He stopped talking, but he did not stop fuming.

"In a matter of minutes, some of you will want to go for my jugular. Resist the urge." Turner took a walk about and when he finished, he offered a laugh at the Gang's expense. "The men and women in this room have risen to the highest levels in their chosen fields. You have served at the highest level in our government, and for sundry reasons you have turned your back on your Nation by becoming ancillary leaders in a worldwide criminal syndicate. You are all brilliant, accomplished individuals, and yet not one of you knows a fuck about this organization—you don't even know to whom you've pledged allegiance." Turner ignored the gasps and growls and stared down each person, holding his final glare for Carter Thorndyke when he pronounced, "I am not The Body of The Realm and have never held that position. I have been the conduit between the mastermind and this pitiful Gang."

Carter charged Turner, stopped dead in his tracks when the presidential candidate pointed a handgun and demanded, **"Sit the fuck down, Carter."**

A shiver runs Felicity's spine at the memory, another runs when her phone rings. She answers it with the following words, "Same time and place as last evening." She disconnects.

# Who's in?

Felicity Ferraro enters the room without escort. "Last night was the Turner Rodgers' Show. I'm in charge this evening." She walks to the head of the lengthy conference table. "I suspect the waft of shit coming from your kickers is because Malcolm Price entered the 2020 presidential race, and you realize the aspirations born in this very room 24-hours ago are in jeopardy."

Carter Thorndyke pushes back from the table and walks to the head at the opposite end of Felicity, "Our aspirations aren't in jeopardy, Mrs. Ferraro, they're fucking gone. Turner Rodgers hasn't a fucking chance if he goes toe-to-toe with Malcolm Price." He pauses. He waits for rebuttal. He receives none. "Price getting the White House is the least of our fucking problems, ladies and gentlemen. Curtis Robert Morgan is dead, and it's obvious The Body ordered his assassination, without our knowledge or our consent. That last bit of information will be of no consequence to RFI, the FBI, the CIA, or any other law enforcement agency hunting the assassin of the senior senator from Georgia. When the authorities find the sucker who pulled the trigger on behalf of this organization, and he or she learns The

Realm has disbanded, there's no upside to keeping his or her mouth shut. It's unlikely the assassin knows who The Body is, but he or she might know enough to send the authorities our way. That means the people going down for Morgan's death, and every fucking other thing Mystery Man did, are in this room."

Thorndyke lets that settle before continuing. "Let's recap, shall we? In one day, the Gang's powerbase in a worldwide syndicate and in the U.S. government is fucked. Further, we are on the hook for whatever atrocities were perpetrated by The Realm. I can't speak for the rest of you, but I want a pound of flesh for being manipulated by some mysterious puppeteer and being deceived by a second rate politician and an Irish idiot. I invested time and treasure into The Realm. I waited patiently for the cyber huntresses to be in our possession so we could move on to the Alva phase. I waited patiently for Tango to show a return on my financial investment—I'm still waiting on that shit fest. Last night, I learned The Realm has gone dark. As consolation, I was offered a cabinet position in a Turner Rodgers' administration. Tonight, I know there won't be any fucking prize because there won't be a Turner Rodgers' White House. Consider this fair warning, Mrs. Ferraro, I'm done playing the waiting game. I'm going after what I want."

"And that is?"

"I want to know who The Fucking Body is, and I want your head on a spike."

Felicity laughs. "Tell me, Carter, which of those two things fancies you more? If it's the former, you will never get your puppeteer's name from me, nor will you get it from the man you disparaged a moment ago."

He laughs. "You're a spitfire, I'll give you that, Mrs. Ferraro, but mark my words, there will come a day when you find yourself at my mercy. Again, fair warning, I show no mercy. When I demand answers from you, you'd be wise to give me answers."

Felicity sets her course—or seals her fate—when she stares down the former secretary, "Save your threats, Carter. Before ascending to the role of conduit in The Realm, this Irish idiot was The Fixer for the lot of you. I know where every bone of criminality perpetrated by everyone in this room is buried. You'd be well advised to ignore the misguided belief that dead women don't talk. I assure you, should anything happen to me, your files will be in the hands of the FBI, DOJ, and RFI within 48-hours of my being reported missing. Come to think of it, Carter, purely for shits and giggles, your set of incriminating documents will also be sent to the secretary of Homeland Security. Men and women, do not push me, and don't ever threaten me. I am the only person in this room who knows the identity of The Body, and I assure you I have been afforded certain protections for keeping you in the dark and in line. Now shut the fuck up, get the fuck out, and if you chose to speak about The Realm, The Body, or members of the Gang, your words will be the last you ever speak, so make them count."

The Gang files past without comment. Thorndyke pulls up the rear and fills the doorway for many seconds. "Watch your back, Felicity, because I'm coming for you."

Turner Rodgers enters the room through a back doorway, "For your sake, Felicity, I hope you aren't bluffing about having protections because every Gang member wants you dead."

"For your sake, Turner, I hope you win the election, otherwise you'll be dead." She pushes past him and makes her way out one door, while he leaves through the other.

The Gang waits for the meeting room to empty before convening an emergency session. Carter Thorndyke is in charge and enraged. "The Realm started to hit the shits after the Paul Ferraro killings of Abigail Forrester, Celia Brettenvue, Dominique Brettenvue, and Stacy Remington. Within days of those killings, Mystery Man had the son of Rocco Fiancetti murdered inside Stacy Remington's townhouse. Within days of that colossally stupid decision, the Remington and Reynolds townhouses were burned to the ground." Thorndyke lets his words set a bit before laying things bare.

"Destroying the FICA director's home made perfect sense. Torching Attorney Reynold's place did not make sense—at first. Then I remembered the bombshell announcement Mathis Reynolds made at Stacy Remington's funeral, that they had been secretly married for more than a decade. Supposedly, those two **very** different people found one another, fell in love, and married. More likely, Reynolds pursued Remington, not to capture her heart, but to gain access to classified FICA information. As far as I'm concerned, that explains one part of our mystery, now for the other part. What better way to keep an eye on us than to have a family member be part of the Gang." He waits for the attendees to catch up.

"I see we've all come to the same conclusion. I've had people checking on the whereabouts of Mathis and Eli Reynolds for weeks. Both men are in the wind. Initially, I assumed Eli was off the grid in a show of support for his widowed brother, but it's been months since either of them have been seen or heard from. There is no question in my mind that Mathis Reynolds is The Body, and he insulated himself by using Turner Rodgers and Eli Reynolds as go-betweens and handlers." Thorndyke lets his words and the ramifications of those words settle. "We need irrefutable proof about the Reynolds brothers. We can't get shit from them, so we need to get our information from Rodgers or Ferraro. One of those two people might get lucky and land his ass in the Oval, so he's untouchable. That leaves the bitch."

"What good will it do us at this point to know who The Body is?" two Gang members ask.

"Risk management. There are too many people outside this room who know about our involvement in The Realm. We need to neutralize every one of them. We're starting with Felicity Ferraro, then we get Jack McGovern, if he's still alive. Then we find Mathis and Eli Reynolds. If we don't fuck them, they will fuck us. None of us knows jack about The Body or what he has been doing behind the scenes. Whatever it is, you can bet the fucking farm that the people in this room are going to take the fall. The Body played us brilliantly, with the help of Turner Rodgers, Eli Reynolds, and Felicity Ferraro. It's time to even the score. Who's in?"

## Missing Children

RFI Security Specialist, Mike Monopoli, watched The Widow leave the **Swill on the Hill**, a five-star bar and grill famous for a Pulled Political Pork sandwich plate served with a side of Yankee Noodle Salad and pint of Sam Adams beer. Mike didn't follow The Widow from the parking lot; he didn't need to. He already GPS trapped her burgundy Lexus RX 350 and had Joy Fiancetti, head of cyber security at Rocco Fiancetti Incorporated, tap into the installed video and audio cameras inside the Ferraro home. Mike keeps one eye on the Lexus as it moves from DC to Maryland and the other eye on the eatery's front door. "I know where you are and what you're doing, Mrs. Ferraro. Let's see if I can figure out what you were doing inside the restaurant. It wasn't eating, that's for sure." He waits nearly an hour before his patience pays off. Faces he saw leaving the restaurant the night before exit en masse and walk to cars that line the curb. "The **Swill on the Hill** is good, but not good enough for all these heavy-hitters to be here two nights in a row. I'd say a meeting just adjourned." He grabs his camera and snaps a few pictures, loads them into a facial recognition program to confirm his eyeball identification, sends the file to Joy, and heads to The Widow's house. "Now for the tough part, staying awake through another night of nothingness."

Mike's been on surveillance for three weeks and so far there's been nothing of consequence to report. Still he reports in to Joy every night, "The Widow does nothing and says nothing—although, she whispers from time to time. Her husband is dead, her children are gone, she is no longer employed at Preston and Porter, and if she works for The Realm, there's nothing on this end to support that. She got several cell phone calls earlier and answered none of them. Then she received a call that didn't come in on her landline or her cell, so it must be a burner. She was online for a couple of minutes, saying the word 'yes' only once. A few hours later, she answered a call with, 'same time and place as last evening.' She headed to the **Swill on the Hill**, stayed for nearly an hour, then headed home. Other than that, there's been nothing. Joy, I'll call you back once she's settled in."

He checks his watch and blasts some heat inside his vehicle, "Midnight at the Ferraro estate, and it's fucking brick in Monopoli's car. If history repeats, The Widow will head upstairs in a couple minutes." She does. "She'll go directly to her master." She does not. Mike sits straighter, pulls a set of night vision binoculars, and follows her along the upper hallway as she lights each of her children's rooms. She spends some time inside each, then darkens them. When she enters the master suite and turns off the lights, Mike makes a second call, "Joy, what do we know about the Ferraro kids?"

"I spent the better part of the day staring at the Ferraro Family whiteboard wondering the same thing. Why do you ask?"

"There is zero kid-related activity on this end. They aren't here, and I haven't heard any mention of them. Usually, when she goes upstairs for the night, she goes directly to the master suite. Tonight, she went into each of the kids bedrooms, turned on the lights, and stayed a few minutes. I wonder whether Felicity Ferraro knows where her kids are. She's not getting calls with updates about them, and she's not making any, 'Hey, it's Mommy' calls either."

Joy pulls a long breath. "So much for getting any sleep tonight."

"Hey, Joy, before you go, any news on Fred?"

"The team hasn't heard from him since Senator Morgan's shooting."

"It's been two weeks. How long are we gonna let him fly solo? Hell, we don't even know if he's still flying at all."

"Fred can take care of himself."

"You're tracking him." It could have been a question; it wasn't.

Joy laughs, "No comment. An FYI though, Rocco is heading to Shelby Webber's place to discuss a few things with John. He'll be in Virginia for a few days if you need him. I suppose you heard about Malcolm entering the race?"

"I'm in the DC radio-sphere, so yeah I heard. Fucking brass balls on that guy."

"Rocco was at the services when Malcolm announced his candidacy. He said he could feel the shake of fear run the Cathedral."

"I bet. Listen Joy, since The Widow is in for the night, I'm going back to DC to get a pulled pork sandwich and a side of noodle salad."

"Mmm. I could use a sandwich. Talk soon."

Joy disconnects, puts on her robe, and heads back to the Computer Center. She stares at the Ferraro Family whiteboard for several minutes and wonders aloud, "Do you know where your children are, Mrs. Ferraro? I don't think you do." Joy calls Annie, "Sorry for the late call, but can you bring a major caffeine fix and plate of food to the Center? I've got a long night of work ahead. And if you want to go diving, bring some food and drinks for yourself."

Annie arrives twenty minutes later, her fingers ready to smoke a keyboard or two. "Who are we going down on?"

Joy laughs.

"Did I say *down on*?"

"You did."

"Meant to say, who are we going deep on?"

Joy laughs.

"Not much better?"

"Nope."

"Why am I here, Joy?"

"We're going down and deep on The Widow."

"What are we looking for?"

"Her kids."

"Really? The Widow doesn't know where her kids are?"

"She doesn't know where they are, but I think she knows who they're with."

"And who's that?"

"My guess is Mathis Reynolds."

"Interesting choice of babysitter."

"Doubt she had any say in the decision."

"That can't be good. Let's get to work."

Joy offers Annie a place to start. "Mike said Felicity Ferraro got a call earlier today. It wasn't on her landline or her cell, so we won't get much on today's call, but concentrate on cell activity from the date of Paul Ferraro's arrest through today. Look at everything, but isolate and trace blocked or no name numbers. And make sure you use your spare signature, Annie."

Before Joy finishes half a sandwich, Annie's fingers hit pay dirt.

"I've got some video texts."

"Send them to the overhead screen."

Video #1: Four-year-old twins are sitting on a rock at the water's edge, surrounded by a lush forest. The tykes are dressed for a day of woodland exploring with little binoculars hanging from their necks, and wide-brimmed hats covering their heads. Rainboots with cartoon frogs and turtles show signs of recent water play. The boy and girl are holding their tiny hands in the air and waving to the camera. Their little singsong voices calling out, "Hi, Mommy. We love you."

Video #2: Four-year-old twins are moving back and forth on swings affixed to a thick tree branch, their tiny bottoms barely causing a bend in the black rubber seats, and their kicking legs pump off-rhythm. They squeal in delight as they sing, "Push, please, high, high."

Video #3: Four-year-old twins are straddling brand new bikes with training wheels, front baskets, and handlebar streamers. The tots' helmets are fastened tight under their chins, still they flop a bit to the side when they wave to the camera. "Thank you, Mommy. We saved you a piece of cake. We love you, Mommy."

Video #4: A man's legs are stretched beyond a low chair on a sandy beach that welcomes gentle rolling waves from a vast blue ocean. It's clear the man is recording the activities around him. The camera moves slowly, capturing images of four adorable children frolicking at the water's edge.

They are slathered in sunscreen and have caked, wet sand on nearly every part of their tiny bodies. Their giggles and squeals of delight lift to the world around them. The man calls out, "We're making a video for Mommy. Say hello to Mommy, and tell her you love her." Singsong voices become part of a symphony of splashing water and calling birds. The sights and sounds continue for a minute, then the screen fades to black.

Joy calls Annie's mother and leaves a message, **"Sorry for the late hour, Kitt, but I'd like you to get coverage for Joseph after breakfast and join Annie and me in the Computer Center. Sleep well."** Joy watches the video texts again, "Annie, we'll get your mother's thoughts on the kids while you and I pull apart the topography. Mathis Reynolds has the Ferraro children. We find them, we find him. Get some sleep, and be back here by 8 AM."

# Snowfall Prison

Eli Reynolds has been in a foul mood for nearly a week, and it's only getting worse. He's taken to yelling at Leavy for no cause, denying her requests for outdoor time, and moving about the cabin in a very menacing way. Leavy is currently chained to the comfort room couch, desperate to go to the second-floor loft, but too afraid to ask. Her silent mantra, *Whatever it takes,* is on a continuous loop now. When her captor steps outside to make a call, she breathes deeply and tries to settle her nerves. She is pretending to read when Eli storms into the cabin and directly toward her. She scrambles from the couch and moves away only to be caught tight by the chain on her ankle.

He grabs her wrist, "Don't ever move away from me, Leavy." He pushes her against the nearest wall, her head hitting hard. He rips open her flannel shirt and is starting on her pants when his phone rings, "Don't move from this spot," he warns.

He takes the ringing phone and before he gets out of the log cabin he starts talking, "What the fuck is going on, Mathis?" The younger Reynolds brother storms back inside and finds Leavy heaped on the floor moaning. He quickly moves to her side, pulls her bloody hand away from her head. "Shit!" He feels around the bleeding gash and finds an egg-sized knot very near the area of her first head injury. "Leavy."

She moans.

He runs from the room to get his medical kit.

She smiles, then winces in pain.

*Still off the grid.*

Fred

The RFI detective hasn't spoken with anyone from his team in two weeks, nor has he packed away the failure of missed clues and unpulled threads that resulted in the death of a great man. Fred steps out of his rental, leans a butt cheek and follows the painful trajectory from "a lake to a river..."

Ted Brothers nudged Fred's shoulder as a thick man with thick neck carrying a thick attitude and a big-ass gun approached. "Haven't seen you two before," he gruffed.

"We're here for Layne Osterman."

Thick Man faltered a tiny step, "That so?"

Fred nodded.

"Haven't seen Layne since my active duty days and haven't got your names yet, gentlemen."

Fred ignored. "That's Layne's cherry red Camaro sitting close to your house."

"That so?"

"Don't see your black F-150 anywhere, Sergeant Noone. I suspect we'll find it when we find Layne. And make no mistake, we will find her, and when we do, your ass is gonna be riding a prison bench with her."

Fred turned to leave and called over his shoulder, "When you talk to Layne, tell her Fred Serpico and the whole Rocco Fiancetti Incorporated team is looking for her."

Sergeant Adam Noone called over his shoulder, "We won't be talking until she's done with her mission, and you and your fucking RFI team won't figure this shit out until it's too late, Serpico."

Fred kicks a stone, then another. He thinks about moving on, but he makes himself push through the worst of it. "That's the Blue Marsh Lake part, now for the Moon River part..."

Mama Girl found Fred stretched the length of the leather couch by the windows, eyes wide open and fixed on the ceiling. She touched his face and he shot up straight.

"Good, no need to call the county coroner. Get yourself in the kitchen now, boy. And no talking back."

Fred did as he was told.

Mama Girl handed him a glass of orange juice, "Drink."

Fred did as he was told.

She handed him a bowl of cereal, "Eat. When you're done, get outside for some fresh air and into a shower for a fresh smell, then you'll right yourself." She turned and walked away.

On his second loop around and through Hufnagle Park, he was still thinking about Mama Girl. "Tough broad, bossy broad, gritty broad raising her son all by herself. Doing things no woman should have to do. Times were different back then, still Mama Girl was alone. Mama Girl was alone!" A memory banged the fuck out of his head. He hauled ass across the snow-covered park and darted across the street ignoring the blare of horns. "No. No. No." He slammed his hand on the call button for the privacy elevator and jumped up and down impatiently waiting for it to arrive. "No. No. No." He threw himself out of the vertical ride and into the great room, startling Mama Girl. He raced to the master bedroom and threw open the door, members of his team following tight on his heels.

Malcolm and Gretchen bolted from the bed.

"MALCOLM! CALL CUTRIS. GRETCHEN CALL MADISON. THE SNIPER IS GOING AFTER THE SENATOR. CALL! CALL! JESUS, CALL!"

The senator's phone buzzed on the counter in his waterfront estate. Madison answered when she saw the name on the display, "Hello, Malcolm."

"MADISON FIND MY FATHER! HE'S IN DANGER!"

Madison rushed to the wrap-porch and to Curtis' prone form, "MALCOLM, HE'S BEEN SHOT."

"Fred, he's shot," Malcolm groaned.

"Ted, Granger, call 9-1-1! Get help! River's Bend!" Fred grabbed the phone from Malcolm's hand, "Madison, it's Fred Serpico, are you with him?"

"Yes."

"Is there a pulse?"

"Yes."

"Is he breathing?"

"Yes."

"Fucking Noone was right, I didn't figure the shit out until it was too late." He bangs his hand against the car, winces in pain, turns his palm over and eyes the bruise that's spreading wide and deepening in color. "Need. To. Stop. Banging. My. Fucking. Hand." He wraps his throbbing palm around an ice cold soda can before pulling a good, long swig. "I'm figuring shit out now, asshole—too late for Morgan, but I've got Layne Osterman in my sights and I'm gonna bring her the fuck in, then I'm gonna bust the fuck out of you, Noone." The beep of Layne's GPS gets the detective's attention pretty quick. "Looks like the Pick Two tryst is over, now what?" He gets into his car, hangs back, tracks her GPS coordinates and when she stops, he checks the internet. "Phil's Auto Sales and Other Stuff. Looks like Assassin Babe is ready to ditch the F-150, which means she'll be ditching my GPS. I'm fucked unless I can do another slap-and-tack. Time to get some help from my team." Fred grabs his cell and starts by listening to his voicemail messages expecting another round of **'get in touch' … 'just checking in' … 'let us know you're okay.'** This time Fred doesn't get what he expects; he gets what he needs.

"Fred, it's Ted. This isn't a get-in-touch-with-me call. I figure you're riding Layne Osterman. Don't know how you found her, but statistical probabilities suggest you found her on her way to Noone's place after the kill. If you're not bringing her in, you must think she's gonna take you to Alaska. Let me know when you're in the 49th state."

Fred smiles wide, "Will do, Poindexter."

"Fred, it's Joy. Hope you're enjoying your cross-country road trip. Here's an update: nothing more from Leavy. Your team is still trying to figure out what the sniper-needle was doing in the Alaskan-haystack for three months. As for The Widow, Mike is on her 24/7 and Annie, Kitt, and I are working an angle that involves Mathis Reynolds and the Ferraro kids. I'll check back in in a few, and by the way, John and Shelby still don't know Layne Osterman killed Senator Morgan. It's getting hard keeping it from them, so get on with it."

Fred smiles and plays along, "Working on it, Joy."

"Fred, it's John. If you've gone dark because you're tailing Morgan's assassin, shit is going to hit hard when Director Webber finds out. She is **not** going to appreciate being left out of the loop on this. She can, and she will, have the FBI track your ass and throw it in jail, so I suggest you get on with it, as Joy would say. Reach out when you need help."

Fred bangs out a text first: **Kittridge, might miss our phone call tonight. I heard you're working something with Annie and Joy. Good luck. Be in**

**touch when I can. Sing a Beatles tune to our boy and his baby sister (just a feeling). Miss you.** He presses Send and makes a call. "John, I need a favor."

John Maxwell does something he's not wont to do—he laughs. "Are you in lockup somewhere? If posting bail is the favor, then forget it."

"No lockup yet. I'm on the tail of the assassin. The vehicle that was used during the hit was just traded in at Phil's Auto Sales and Other Stuff on Industrial Road, north of Morgantown, West Virginia. It sure would help if the FBI could pay Phil a visit and impound the shit out of that vehicle."

"That all, Fred?"

"Nope. Find out what the Other Stuff is all about, would ya?"

"For real?"

"Have to tell you, John, I'm a bit curious," Fred laughs.

"Is that all, Fred?"

"Nope. The F-150 belongs to former Army Sergeant Adam Noone. He owns High Noone firing range up at Blue Marsh Lake in Pennsylvania. If you contact him about the truck sale, he'll tip off the assassin and I'll lose her. That can't happen, John. She's leading me to Leavy."

"Fuck, Fred. You want the FBI to help, but you don't want the FBI to do its job."

"I know I'm putting you in the middle, but it's Leavy."

"I'll put a lid on this for as long as I can. Anything else?"

"Just one thing, when I give the okay and you make a move on Sergeant Noone, there should be a cherry red Camaro at his place. That's the car Benton Brettenvue boosted on his way out of Philly the night Celia was killed. My sniper drove it for a while, so her fingerprints and those of Brettenvue should be all over it."

"When I pull her prints, what will I learn?"

"They belong to Layne Osterman of Beaver Falls, Pennsylvania. She served with Eli Reynolds, Paul Ferraro, and Mason Trellis in a ranger unit and is the most recently hired assassin of The Realm."

"As usual, Fred, good work. Really good work. When did you ID Osterman?"

"We got a positive on her a few days before the assassination of Senator Morgan, but she was in the wind by then. I was on the phone with Madison Morgan seconds after the senator was shot ....... I just couldn't find the thread in time. I've been tailing Osterman ever since. I'm hoping she leads me to Eli and Leavy. I'm sorry about keeping you in the dark, John. Since I haven't spoken with anyone at RFI in weeks, they have deniability with you and Shelby. I need to be the one to bring Morgan's killer in."

"Yeup. Leave your phone on so I can reach you when this shit blows up in my face."

"Will do. Thanks, John."

## Layne

Assassin Babe pulls from the West Virginia lot of Phil's Auto Sales and Other Stuff in a brand new 2019 gray Chevy Tahoe, the same make and model as the one she used to own, the one that's currently holding the charred remains of Benton Brettenvue in Beaver Falls. She fiddles with dials on the dash, adjusts her rearview and sideview mirrors, then settles deep into the heated seat before hopping onto the highway.

Fred follows her to the interstate and lets her get far enough away before pursuing. He calls John, "I'm following a 2019 gray Chevy Tahoe, WV plates 1HO628 up Interstate 68. I haven't trapped the vehicle, so standby. I'll give you coordinates along the way, but if I lose her, be ready to make the arrest of the century."

Fred tracks Layne from West Virginia to the Illinois stateline without benefit of GPS. Nine plus hours of squinting at a set of tail lights has left the man in desperate need of food, sleep, and the opportunity to trap her new ride. He waits at a coffee drive-thru until the fugitive checks into a cheap motel and turns off the room's light. He parks in a dark corner of the parking lot, unfolds himself from the seat, steps his numb feet onto the ground, stretches every muscle, moves silently to the beautiful new ride of Layne Osterman and GPS traps the hell out of it.

He hits the head in a small restaurant attached to the motel, grabs some food to go, and prepares for a nice long nap in the back seat of the rental he's really beginning to hate. "Just one more thing before nighty-night. I need to set my wake-up call." He places a beer bottle underneath the Chevy's right front tire. "That should do it." Before he closes his eyes, he sends a text to Ted Brothers.

**From Fred: 21st state**

# THE BODY

Mathis Reynolds is sitting on a sweeping veranda one step down from a sweeping villa on a white sandy beach in Australia. He is working, which essentially means he is reading everything written about the assassination of Curtis Morgan and the political ascension of the dead senator's son, Malcolm Price. "Audacious move declaring your candidacy and taking your father's place before anyone else claimed it. And announcing your intentions in front of a captive audience—brilliant move, Mr. Price. By the time the last church bells tolled, a grieving son had laid claim to his father's political power. Well played, indeed."

The pseudo-father of the Ferraro children gets off his chaise and answers their call for a beach race, "Off you go. I'll catch up in no time." He closes his laptop, leaves it behind, and moves on, his next plan nearly in place. "You will get the White House, Mr. Price, and I will get what I want, what I have always wanted—Alva."

He waves his hand, "I'll be with you as soon as I make a call."

*Friendly waves
and requests for immunity.*


Felicity has been at her kitchen counter staring at a darkened computer screen since the vibration of her phone woke her from a sound sleep. The Body delivered his message, then hung up. Her head has been a riot of thoughts and questions since then. The Widow knows she's being watched by him and by the man outside. She struggles to find something to tether her, to deter her. "Nothing. There's nothing. I can't do this any longer. My children are gone. I have no idea where they are and no one to help me find them. I could hire people to track them, but I don't know who works for The Body, and I might walk into a trap. Besides, who could tackle this challenge? Who has the necessary resources or brass balls to take on Mathis Reynolds?" A thought flashes. "Maybe there is someone who could help, someone who has an incentive to help. She is a powerful woman and perfectly suited to the challenge, but would she be inclined to help me? No, but she might help my children." A new thought starts banging.

Mike snaps to and sits straight at the sound of Felicity Ferraro's voice.

"Time to throw out the trash," she laughs a bit. "I sound a bit mad, but is there any wonder I'm talking to myself? Nope." Seconds later the garage door opens, and the Lexus backs the length of the driveway. The Widow gives a wide smile and friendly wave to the RFI specialist who's been caught totally off guard. Mike returns her wave and follows close behind. He leans forward, trains his eye on the driver's side window as it lowers, on her hand as it reaches out, on the object that is dropped to the ground. The Widow toots her horn twice, waves her hand, closes her window, and speeds off. Mike pulls to a stop and retrieves the discarded object. He calls his boss, "Are you still at Director Webber's?"

"Si."

"Be waiting outside. ETA a half-hour to a half-day depending on DC traffic."

The 51-year-old Italian Stallion is outside Shelby's house waiting in frigid air. His shoulder is leaning against the house, his hands are tucked deep into his overcoat, and his stare is locked on the Potomac River.

Mike gives a quick tap of the horn.

Rocco hops onto the passenger seat and puts on the latex gloves Mike hands him. The former MI6 senior special operative opens a plastic sandwich bag, removes a folded piece of paper and reads: **I know everything. I want full immunity.**

"The Widow?"

"Yeah. After weeks of silence, she got up really early this morning, mumbled a bunch of shit, then said it was time to throw out the trash.

In a matter of seconds, she was behind the wheel of her Lexus and backing down the driveway. She caught my ass totally off guard, threw me a wide smile, a friendly wave, and let me know she enjoyed every damned bit of it. I followed along, and a quarter mile from her place, she lowered the driver side window, put her hand out, and dropped that plastic bag onto the ground. Then she tooted her horn, waved her hand, and drove off."

Rocco puts the paper back into the plastic bag and tucks it into the inside breast pocket of his overcoat. "The Widow wants something."

"Immunity."

"Something other than immunity. Felicity Ferraro is a brilliant attorney. She knows RFI can't offer her immunity, only the U.S. government can. If she dropped this note thinking you are with the FBI, then she wants immunity. If she thinks you are with RFI, she wants something only we can provide. Either way, she's playing us. Her morning contact with you appears impulsive, but it was planned."

Mike gives a shake of his head.

"You are of disagreement, Master Michael."

"The Widow is missing her kids, Rocco. A broken mother might act impulsively."

"Si. Felicity Ferraro is a mother, but foremost she is a cunning woman, and if we are correct, she sits on the leadership level of The Realm. And if she reports to Mathis Reynolds and he has her children, getting help behind his back is a deadly move." Rocco pats his breast pocket, "This note should be given consideration, but we haven't much time for contemplation. We need to make an immediate strike. RFI will kidnap The Widow, bring her to The Compound, and figure this out later."

"Of course we will," Mike's words drip with resignation.

Rocco laughs big.

*PB&Justice.*

Ted Brothers finds Randy and Penny with mouthfuls of sandwiches—he PB, and she PB&J. "Good work getting the 8th floor changed back to campaign space and the 7th floor set as the new RFI Diving Center. As soon as you're done eating, I need you to push harder on Layne Osterman. I got a text from Fred—"

"Thank, God. I was starting to worry."

"Not me. I figured he found some big-ass window and couldn't pull himself away."

Penny snorts a bit of milk from the long pull she took, and after a wipe or two, she asks, "Did Fred say where he's been?"

"No, but he's in Illinois, and he thinks Osterman might be moving toward Alaska. That's our hope, anyway."

Penny stuffs her last bite and pushes from the table, "We need to find something on Layne Osterman's time in Alaska to help Fred. The woman was there for three months. She stayed somewhere, ate somewhere, and she might have been with someone. We haven't found anything through real estate records, but there's gotta be something that will shed some light. Gentlemen, I'm pulling a Fred Serpico and parking my ass in front of those windows right there to do some intense processing. I expect quiet from the two of you."

"Oh, Jesus," the men say in unison.

Skidaway, Georgia

Malcolm Price has been at the home of the widowed Morgan since he declared his candidacy at the Washington National Cathedral. His pronouncement has drawn strong support from the liberal camps and expected criticism from the conservative camps. Malcolm Price doesn't care about external noise; he cares only about accompanying his father to his final resting place at the Bonaventure Cemetery in a plot near the scenic Wilmington River.

For the past many hours, Malcolm has been standing in the spot where his father stood when he was cut down. Malcolm's eyes are locked on the land across Moon River, "One shot. That's all it took to end a man's life, to rip apart a family so new and tender, to crush a man's dreams, a son's needs." When he's chilled deep and near broken, he walks the path to his father's office. He knuckle-raps once, hoping to hear his father's call. Malcolm enters the quiet chamber, silently walks his father's space, ponders at the window overlooking the river his dad loved dearly, then sits in the visitor's chair, the one he used the day he met his father...

"When did you first learn you are my father?"

"In 2003, when you turned pro. I read an article on you, and it mentioned Bertha's name."

"Did my mother tell you about the pregnancy?"

**The man pulled a deep breath and released it slowly.** "Sadly, no. On our last day together, Bertha was troubled by something. She asked for some time alone, and like a damned fool, I gave it to her. When I returned to our place, she was gone. I hired a private investigator who tracked her to the Sackville projects. People who knew her said she was long gone. A year after she left me, I was moving out of the apartment where she and I spent our time. I found a calendar that she used to document our lives together—apparently, she documented her menstrual cycle in that calendar, too. That's the day I found out about the missed period—instead of telling me about the pregnancy, she ran."

"And in 2003, when I went pro, did you think about contacting us?"

**The man nodded, then shook his head.** "At that time, I was congressman out of the 1st District of Georgia with my sights set on becoming senator. I had my private investigator take a look into your lives. Dolan learned some things about your mother..." **the Senator stopped and looked at Malcolm, unsure if he should continue.**

"Senator, I know of those things. Speak freely."

"I'm not shielding you from those things, Malcolm. I'm shielding myself from thinking about all of the things Bertha did to support you, and to protect me."

**Malcolm waded into the unsettled waters,** "What did my mother protect you from?"

"Myself. I would have given everything I had, or ever would have had, for Bertha."

**Malcolm scoffed,** "She said those exact words about you."

"Because they are true. Your mother left me that day because had our illicit affair become known, it would have cost me everything, perhaps even my freedom. Instead of letting me suffer the consequences of my actions, she left me with everything and took nothing in return." **The Senator stared at his Moon River,** "I was allowed to have all of this because your mother loved me."

Malcolm allowed the man his quiet moments of reflection and took a few for himself. He walked the room, surveyed pieces of a personal and professional history, all richly framed and proudly displayed: educational degrees, congressional and senatorial headshots, newspaper articles of note, and family photographs. The man with no paternal history, leaned in and studied a picture of Senator Curtis Robert Morgan standing with his father, Senator Robert Mayfield Morgan. Malcolm recognized the smile on the men's faces as his own. *My blood*, he silently reflected and accepted. He strolled back toward the fine reproduction of the writing desk used by

President George Washington, upon which sat two things: a bumper sticker that read, Curtis Morgan for President – 2020, and a copy of the central Pennsylvania newspaper, *Liberty Rings*.

"Senator, what about your plans? Will you still run for President?"

The Senator shook his head, "Not likely."

So lost in thought, Malcolm jumps at the touch of his wife's hand on his shoulder. "Gretchen, I didn't hear you come in."

"It's time to leave for the cemetery. Do you need anything?"

"Justice for my father."

# Snowfall Prison

Leavy is sporting a handful of stitches across a sizeable egg on the back of her head. She knows she went overboard when she smacked her noggin against the wall, but she still thinks her head injury is better than the rape that awaited her at the hands of her captor. Within minutes of Eli finding Leavy, he performed a concussion assessment. Having been down that road with 'Dr. Eli' before, Leavy exaggerated her symptoms and degree of confusion. It worked like a charm. The medic diagnosed a borderline grade 2-3 concussion, and though the injury kept her under his watchful eye, he made no sexual demands.

*Still off the grid.*

# Fred

The detective is woken by the beep of GPS, orients himself, then checks the dashboard clock, "Nine." The detective has taken to parking and sleeping miles away from whatever sleazebag hotel Assassin Babe hangs her holster. He waits until she gets her car out on the road, then heads to the nearest restaurant for some food, coffee, and a piss. When he's fed, caffeinated, and drained, he puts the rental in drive and starts humming a little Seger and assessing his mark, "Layne Osterman is in survival mode. She's traveling at night and sleeping during the day. I figure I'm in for eight or so hours of road." He grabs his cell from the passenger seat, "Let's see if my woman can keep me company. I miss you," he says as soon as she answers.

"You usually wait until the end of our conversation before you go all sweet, what's up?"

"Wanted to make sure I didn't forget to tell you. You sound good, Kittridge."

"I am good. I'm working with Candace at the firing range, and with Joy and Annie at the

Computer Center, and I had a breakthrough or an epiphany or whatever, so things are better."

Fred smiles wide.

"You're smiling wide, aren't you?"

"You bet I am. Should I be asking about the firing range, the breakthrough, the epiphany, or the whatever?"

"We'll talk when you get home."

"Home? Don't think I ever heard you call The Compound home before."

"Like I said, things are better."

"Still smiling, Kittridge. How's our boy and our bun?"

"Wonderful. You think we're having a girl bun, or do you want a girl bun?"

"I want you, Kittridge. I want us. Whoever else joins our family is along for an incredible ride. Tell me what's going on at RFI?"

"Everyone is relieved to know you're still amongst the living. It was really difficult keeping our communications secret."

"I know, Kittridge. I just needed…"

"No explanations. I'm just glad their minds are eased. Joy's tracking you, and she lets everyone know where you are … you're heading northwest toward Alaska, right?"

"Right."

"Joy said she picked you up when you turned your cell on."

"Yeah, she's been tracking me the whole time."

"How?"

"She tapped into your phone. She knew I'd never leave you hanging, Kittridge."

"I knew that too, Fred."

"I know, babe."

"I'm keeping your bed warm, Fred."

"Damn, Kittridge, I miss you."

"You already said that."

"Deserves repeating. Sorry to cut this short, but the assassin is picking up speed. I'll call tomorrow. And Kittridge, I'm happy."

*Lucky centesimo.*


Penny is flat on her back, her arm slung across her eyes. Short, soft groans barely cut the stillness of the room. She's awake from her nap and has called out to Ted and Randy several times, but both men are at the 7th floor Diving Center. Out of frustration she curses the absent Fred Serpico, "You could have warned me about winter-window-watching and subsequent snow blindness, oh, Detecting One!"

Ted and Randy laugh as they make their way in, "I guess processing in front of wall to wall glass takes some practice."

"Who knew?" she grunts.

Her man runs his hand along her draped arm and squeezes her fingertips, "Feeling any better, Lucky?"

She groans.

"Did you come up with anything during your perch and ponder?"

"A theory."

"Yeah? What?"

"I'm temporarily blind, and I'm wasting my time."

The mathematician detective corrects, "Part of your theory is fact; the other is conjecture."

Penny groans.

"You hungry?" Randy calls from the kitchen.

"I could use a little something, but you'll have to talk me through my dinner plate."

"This could be fun," Randy laughs when Ted joins him.

"Put the yogurt back, you know she hates it."

"Like I said, this **could** be fun." The ensuing game of Dinnertime Dastardly is halted by Penny's call.

"Ted! Randy!"

The men race from the kitchen, "What!"

"Hospitals, medical clinics, doctors' offices. Osterman was in Alaska for three months, if she twisted an ankle or got fucking snow blindness, she'd need to seek medical attention. Randy go check."

The Kid sprints away muttering, "That damn window has powers! Got a problem, a question, go ponder at that damn window. It's like oracle glass, I tell you."

An hour later, Randy joins Ted and a sitting Penny, who's opened her very bloodshot eyes. Randy stops short at the sight, "When you close your balls of fire tonight, Penny, let the words Kenai Peninsula lull you to sleep. Layne Osterman was seen at Kenai Urgent Medical Center on August 15th for treatment of a puncture wound to her foot and a tetanus shot to her shoulder. On the address section on the patient intake form she wrote: visiting out by the lake."

Ted kisses his woman and texts Fred.

**From Ted: Osterman received minor medical care August 15th at Kenai Urgent Medical Center. On patient intake form she listed her address as out by the lake. We're getting close.**

**From Fred: One – there are 3 million lakes in Alaska. Two – call Rocco and update.**


The Compound

Rocco is just back from his trip to Virginia and is about to tell RFI's sniper/security specialist, Steve Phelps, about the recent events with Mike and The Widow when he receives a call from RFI's most recent hire. "Ah, Theodore Brothers, we finally speak."

"I'll keep this brief, Mr. Fiancetti."

"I have no doubt," Rocco laughs.

"Fred asked me to call. Our team places Layne Osterman at the Kenai Urgent Medical Center on Kenai Peninsula on August 15th. We believe the sniper is currently heading in that direction with Fred not too far behind."

"Excellent work, Theodore. Ask Randy to continue with the Osterman diving and to contact Joy regarding another assignment. You and your centesimo will be working with Mike Monopoli on a separate matter. He will be in touch. And please tell Ms. Meehan to say *si* when I contact her about a position at RFI."

"Will do, sir."

Rocco disconnects and slaps Steve on the shoulder, "We need to prepare The Compound for a very special guest."

Steve groans at the memory of the last very special guest to arrive at The Compound— a very dead special guest...

"Tell me again why I had to sit next to a dead guy on a fifteen-hour flight that should have taken five hours tops, escort him to The Compound, and bury him in a grave that was prepared for your son, who is supposedly dead, but is currently pounding a track at the Athletic Center."

Rocco laughed at the Rambling One, "We couldn't call the U.S. authorities about Deputy Director McGovern's death because my entire team would have been stuck stateside being questioned for an eternity. We couldn't destroy his body because we need it as evidence in the event there's blowback on Director Webber."

"See, it makes perfect sense when you say it, Rocco, but I doubt the authorities are going to see things your way when they find out I smuggled a dead guy into Canada." He pushed from his seat, "If you don't mind, there's a long shower in my future. I need to get the stench of the stiff off of me, and then I need to see Maura about getting this other stiff off of me." He laughed. "If you were Fred, you'd get the joke, Rocco."

"I got it, Steve."

65

*Still off the grid.*

Layne

The paid assassin notices a familiar car in the motel parking lot—a way too familiar car. "I've got a fucking tail." The really pissed-off bitch wants to take her gun and take out her tail; the woman who wants to get her ass to Alaska and get laid sets an alternate plan.

Fred

The detective is exhausted and should be sleeping, but he needed a run, so he drove to the hotel parking lot where Assassin Babe spent the night, parked his ride in a far corner, and began working out the kinks and pumping his blood. He's on the third loop of the mile-long access road that leads from the hotel to the highway, and deep into the repetitive slap of his feet when the Tahoe passes him with a toot of the horn and a chuck of the finger from the smiling Assassin Babe.

"Fuck! She made me." Fred spins and charges toward the motel, where he finds his rental Trashed. The. Fuck. Up. All four tires are slashed, the passenger window is busted out, and the GPS trap is on the glass covered passenger seat. He takes a hip on the dented fender and sends a text to Ted.

**From Fred: 40th state. She made me and fucked up my ride. Keep digging. I'm flying into Anchorage as soon as I handle this mess.**

## Layne

For the first time in days, Layne relaxes and enjoys the ride in her brand new Chevy Tahoe. She lets her mind wander to Eli...

She stood just inside the tree line watching for signs of life in the log cabin. She knew someone was nearby, hadn't yet determined whether the interloper was friend or foe. Movement passed the window from inside, "Looks like I've got company. Fucking should have taken my binoculars. Stupid mistake." She shifted her weight off her injured foot. "Goddamn puncture wound. Foot feels like it's on fire." She stepped behind a big-ass tree and removed her vest, turned it inside out to hide the neon bright orange. She parked her ass on a nearby rock and watched. Nearly an hour later, he stepped outside. She pushed off the rock and began hobbling toward the cabin.

"It's about time, Layne," he met her halfway across an open field.

"Eli, give me a shoulder."

"What happened?"

"Stepped on a nail. I went to Urgent Care for a cleaning and a tetanus shot."

**He pulled her into his arms, carried her inside, and set her on the couch.** "Let me see."

"Medic Reynolds, it's way below your skill."

"Even so." **He removed her boot, checked her foot, removed the rest of her clothes, and settled deep.**

**And then she remembers Sarge's warning…**

"You're going into the biggest mission of your life, Ranger. If you don't want to go out with the senator, you need to review your plan, execute each step, and keep your head clear. That means you **need** to get Eli Reynolds the fuck out of your headspace, Layne. When you're done with the senator, you should get the fuck out of the country for a while. Put some time and space between you and your handler." **Sarge took a seat across from her, demanded her attention.** "Osterman. Taking out a sitting U.S. senator is gonna bring the heat, and if you're too close by, you're gonna get burned." **He saw the flash of stupidity cross her face,** "Don't even think about going to Alaska, or trying to find Eli. If the Feds or RFI are onto to you for the sniper kills in Pennsylvania, then they know about your trip to the Anchorage area. Stay the fuck away from there, or you will go down."

"Two things about that, Sarge, I have nowhere else to go. And if Eli is at the Safe House in Alaska, he won't cast a ranger to the wind; he will take me in. And once I'm under the same roof, I'll make sure he'll want to keep me around."

*Or are you just happy to see me?*

Joy is in the Computer Center reading a text from Ted Brothers when Rocco arrives. The two share a moment, a rather intense moment of greeting.

"I heard you got in last night."

"I'm about to get in, mi amore."

"Hmmmm, maybe you should travel more often," Joy pants.

"Maybe we should take the jet for a spin and recreate our first encounter," he says through kisses and touches.

Joy's desire turns the corner to need, and Then. He. Whispers. In. Her. Ear. "RFI is kidnapping The Widow."

She whimpers, then pushes her husband away, "What did you just say? Because I thought you said that RFI is kidnapping Felicity Ferraro. I know my blood supply is currently some place other than in my brain, but still."

Rocco steps forward and swings his arm around Joy's waist before she puts too much space between them. "Reach into my pocket."

She reaches into the left pocket of his G9 wool jacket.

"Wrong pocket." He smiles.

She reaches into the right pocket of his G9 wool jacket.

"Wrong pocket." He smiles wider.

She slides both hands into the pockets of his jeans. "Mmmmm, the one on the left is considerably fuller than the other." She takes hold of her man.

"Wrong pocket," he says on a catching breath.

"Don't care." She unzips his jacket, unbuttons his shirt, moves the material aside and presses them chest to chest.

Rocco walks Joy backwards and presses her against a wall. He makes urgent work of her blouse and bra. She makes urgent work of her pants and his. The time for kisses and touches makes way for entrances and releases, followed by kisses and touches that lead to a slow, heated rebuild of passion. The lovers move to Joy's Computer Center suite where they slowly unwind one another.

Alexandria

Mike makes just enough noise sneaking into Director Webber's house to disturb the resident. The surveillance specialist quickly packs his gear and is rushing toward the stairs that lead outside when he finds John lying in wait, his arms crossed over this chest, his body blocking the top step. He eyes Mike's hands.

"Going somewhere?" He waits for a response—gets none. "No goodbyes? No, thanks for your hospitality?" John asks.

"You need to move."

"I need a lot of things. I'll start with an explanation."

"I can't, John."

The men are at an impasse until John breaks it. "I'll move if you answer one question, and I won't ask you what's in the works."

Mike thinks. Mike nods.

"How many years in a Federal penitentiary will you be doing if you get caught?"

"Too many for Sweet Annie to stick around waiting for me."

John moves more solidly in Mike's way, "Don't do it, son. Whatever it is, don't do it."

The Compound

Rocco is dressing when a call comes in from a hot-under-the-collar John, "Not a good time, Maxwell…"

"Don't care. Whatever you have planned, get Mike out of it."

"Ah. Did Mike ask you to call?"

"No."

"I appreciate your concern, John, but this is Mike's call?" Rocco accepts the silence he receives before continuing. "Is there anything else?"

"You'd better know what you're doing, Rocco." John disconnects and sprints upstairs to begin listening to the audio from the set of ears he slipped into Mike's gear.

Joy pulls on a thick terry cloth robe and joins her husband in front of a cabinet fireplace throwing a gentle warmth. She wraps her arms around him and nestles against his strong, toned back, "Are you putting Mike on the kidnapping?"

"And Ted and Centesimo."

Joy moves in front of Rocco, "You can't be serious. Mike has never handled anything like this for us, and Ted and Penny have never handled anything for us, and Penny doesn't even work for us. Please tell me you have a contingency plan?"

Rocco smiles, "I just spoke to my contingency plan."

"John?" Joy asks with amazement.

"John Maxwell will intervene. He will learn of Mike's plan, and he will take it away from him. John Maxwell will kidnap The Widow for us."

"Rocco. This will put a wedge between John and Mike."

"Si. Especially when John finds out it was Mike's plan," Rocco smiles wide.

Joy shakes her head at the subterfuge, "If John kidnaps The Widow, what makes you think he won't give her to Shelby Webber?"

"I do not know, Gia. Right now, RFI and FBI have an opportunity to work with Felicity Ferraro. The FBI can offer her immunity, RFI can find her kids. John will feel her out, then explain her options. He'll get her to choose between the

73

two options. Her choice will be telling, though suspect."

"You think she's playing us."

"Si."

"I don't like this, Rocco," Joy calls after her retreating husband.

*Peninsulas, plans,
and a glass of Pinot.*

Rocco steps onto the track and waves Manuel and Dr. Weinstock over.

"Four and a half miles and an hour at the firing range," his son pants.

"That is good news. I have better."

"Leavy?"

"We are closing in."

"Alaska?"

"Kenai Peninsula."

Manuel's heart thunders, "How soon is the rescue mission?"

"Fred will inform, but days to weeks if we have luck." He knows this conversation is going to take a turn, so he rounds it first. "My son will want to be on this mission. Opinion, Doctor?"

"If it's days, no; weeks, perhaps."

"In either case, you are on the rescue mission, Weinstock. I have approval of Director Webber. Hannah Leavy is former FBI, the director wants you attending to her physical and mental necessities." Rocco clasps his hand around the back of his son's neck, "Continue your progress. Leavy is going to need you, here or there."

Alexandria
John eavesdrops on Mike's conference call with Ted Brothers and Penny Meehan.

"I'm gonna be calling the two of you to DC within the next three days. Keep your schedules clear."
"What's the assignment?"
"Kidnapping."

The room closes in on John Maxwell. He sprints downstairs and keeps going until he reaches the exercise room on the lower level. He strips off his sweatshirt and hops onto the treadmill surrendering his headspace to the rhythmic slap of his feet. Soon he is talking to himself, and working through the logistics. "Mike can plan an effective kidnap operation, could even pull it off with the right resources and backup. Ted Brothers is a good resource, but the men haven't really worked together, haven't developed a rhythm. For a kidnapping to work, the members need to know what the other is going to do before the other one even knows. And then there's Penny, WTF. She's smart and all, beyond smart, but she doesn't have any training. She's only ever been an Army reservist, for God's sake."

Shelby, who's been watching and listening from the entrance cuts in, "Apparently, you've forgotten that I was an Army reservist, Director Maxwell."

John looks over his shoulder and hops off the treadmill, "You shouldn't listen to people without their knowledge."

"I'm the Director of the FBI. All I ever do is listen to people without their knowledge. So now that you know I'm listening, you'd better tell me what the hell is in the works."

"I will as soon as I formally resign my position at the FBI."

"Why?"

"Saves you the trouble of firing me."

"Uh huh."

"Director Webber, either way, I believe you said my termination from the Bureau is contingent upon an exit interview with my supervisor." He winks and smirks. "Perhaps you'd like to conduct that necessity in the shower?"

"Lead the way, Director Maxwell."

Chevy Chase

Felicity Ferraro is sitting by a fire in her living room, the first she's enjoyed since the day her husband was arrested. She has a near-empty bottle of Pinot on an end table, half of which is dulling her senses, the other half is ebbing her anxiety over her bold move of dropping the note. She swallows the last sip then jumps at the sound of her ringing cell, "Felicity Ferraro," she says with the slightest slur.

"Mrs. Ferraro, this is FICA Director, John Maxwell. I was given your message. Are you still interested in an immunity deal?"

"Yes."

"Are you available to meet at eight tomorrow evening?"

"Yes. Where?"

"My office, at J. Edgar."

"What if I am seen going into the FBI building?"

"Mrs. Ferraro, you started the ball rolling. Furthermore, it is only a matter of days before the FBI moves on members of The Realm. It will serve you well to be first in line."

There is silence for a full minute. "Will Director Webber be in attendance?"

"If it is warranted. Will you be in attendance tomorrow evening, Mrs. Ferraro?"

"Yes."

"Very well. One last thing, Mrs. Ferraro. So that you are ensured your communication is with an authorized agent of the Bureau, our code phrase is, 'goodnight, Mike'. Please say that into the phone, then hang up."

Felicity Ferraro does as she's been asked, "Goodnight, Mike."

The RFI surveillance specialist who's been listening to the call cracks up laughing. He calls Rocco, "The Widow is meeting John tomorrow at 8 PM. He directed her to J. Edgar, but I doubt that's where the meeting will actually take place. I'll be on her 24/7 until the hookup. By the way, John knows about our ruse."

"Si. No doubt. Explain."

"John told The Widow that their code phrase is 'goodnight, Mike'. He made her say it before hanging up."

Rocco laughs big, "I'm about to say the same thing. Goodnight, Mike."

Mike is respecting the brilliance of John Maxwell when he places his call to Ted Brothers. "I want you and Penny in DC by 7 AM."

"For the kidnapping?"

"Sort of."

*Still off the grid.*

Fred

Fred lands at Ted Stevens International Airport in Anchorage, rents a Land Rover, and heads toward Kenai Peninsula. He travels about three hours along the Seward and Sterling highways and pulls off at mile marker 58, where he places a call to Joy for some help. "I'm in Alaska."

"I know where you are, Fred," she chuckles.

He laughs big.

"What's so funny?"

"Rocco must not be able to get away with shit on your watch."

"Doesn't even bother trying," she chuckles again. "As lovely as this conversation is, you must have called for a reason."

"I'm on Sterling highway at mile marker 58. According to Randy's dive, Osterman was treated at Kenai Urgent Medical Care for a foot wound. On the intake form she listed herself as a visitor at the lake. The damned state of Alaska has more than three million lakes, fact not fiction, so using that as your address is like saying you're the needle in one of three million haystacks in the state. Anyway, since she was on Kenai Peninsula Borough at the time, she was most likely referring to Kenai Lake or Skilak Lake. Mile marker 58 sits between the two. I visited both lakes when I lived in Seattle, spent most of my time at Skilak because it's within the Kenai National Wildlife Refuge. If memory serves, there are probably half a dozen campsites on each lake, but I doubt they have winter camping. Have Randy check out the campgrounds, and have him concentrate on cabins located in the area. I know the real estate purchase and rental searches the team did were a bust, but if we get aerials, we can search cabin by cabin if we have to. In the meantime, I'm gonna do a little snowmobile reconnaissance."

"Do you want backup?"

"Are Mike and Steve available?"

"Both in a few days."

"Good. Let's plan on them coming to help with reconnaissance when they can. We've got some time. Layne ditched me in South Dakota; she still had Wyoming, Idaho, and Washington to travel. That's about 3,000 miles, or five days the way she's been moving through. I'll spend four days looking around the lake. Maybe I'll get lucky. If not, I'll park my ass at mile marker 58 and wait for her to lead me to the safe house. By the way, who's on the rescue team?"

"Besides you, there's Steve, Mike, and Dr. Weinstock."

"Manuel's benched."

"Yes."

"Can't imagine that's sitting well."

"Nope. Your partner's made real progress, but the search and rescue is thousands of miles from here, and Leavy is probably in backcountry Alaska."

"Okay, your call."

"Rocco's call. Hey, Fred, when you get back I want to talk to you about Rocco and—"

"Mathis Reynolds?"

"Yeah. And did you know that we're expecting a guest at The Compound?"

"Nope."

"The Widow is planning an unexpected stay with us."

There is silence, a long period of silence, "Shit, I wish I had a window to look out. I need to process that shit."

Joy cracks up, "You have a windshield, Fred."

"Windshields just don't work for kidnappings. Who's going down for this if the shit hits the fan?"

"John."

Fred laughs big—really big, "John Maxwell doing 25 years in a Federal penitentiary might be fun to watch. Maybe we can get him a bunk in Roland Gaffney's cell."

"Not funny, Fred."

"Look, John's the only one who can pull this off, and he'll do it his own weird way." Fred laughs again then adds, "Dealing with Assassin Babe in the wilds of Alaska is looking pretty good right about now. When you can, let me know what The Kid finds out about camps and cabins and what Federal pen John ends up in. I'll stop for a visit on my way home."

## Layne

Assassin Babe is feeling pretty damned good now that the asshole tail has been sidelined. "Wish I shot the muthafucka, but a girl's gotta do, what a girl's gotta do. And right now, this girl's gotta get to Alaska and do Eli." The contract killer laughs a bit then let's her mind get lost in the hum of her wheels and the thrill of the kill...

She pulled her cell from beneath her pillow, checked caller ID, "Eli" She slid from bed and from behind a closed bathroom door, she whispered, "It's been a while."

"The organization is restructuring. I'm your boss now. We're down two assassins, so you're being bumped up."

"Yes, sir."

"I need you in Philadelphia to take out two people."

"Yes, sir."

"Get rid of Benton Brettenvue, first. We don't need him. Let me know when you're in Philly. Two days tops, Osterman."

"Yes, sir."

Layne gently opened the bathroom door—Benny was waiting for her on the other side.

"Who were you talking to?" he snarled.

"My Daddy," Layne said as she tried to move past him.

"At three in morning?" he blocked her exit.

"He's stink-ass drunk and going on about all the time I'm taking away from the store. Even drunk, the old coot has a point. I come home after a three-month stay in Alaska and immediately shack up with you. I've barely set foot in the store since the day you came in to buy all your gear. I listened to the old man's rage, then agreed to work for the next few days."

Layne tried to get past Benton, again. He didn't budge. "I've explained about the call, Benny, now step the fuck back, you're starting to piss me off."

"Good, I like a bitch who fights back."

"Then you're gonna love this." Before his next blink, she kneed him in the balls, jumped over him as he dropped, pulled his head back by his hair, placed one arm around his neck and her dominant hand across his forehead, lifted herself a up to get leverage, then twisted Benton Brettenvue's head to coincide with her downward trajectory. Layne heard and felt the snap, let him fall dead away, then checked his jugular. "You should have stepped out of my way, Benny." She hopped over his body, pulled a dress on over her head, a pair of boots onto her feet, grabbed her things, hung the *No Maid Service* tag on the outside motel door, grabbed the keys to Benny's Camaro, and got the fuck out of Beaver Falls. As soon as she was beyond the town limits, she called her Daddy.

"It's 3 AM, Sugar, someone better be dead."

"Someone is. Room 11 at the motel. The body needs to disappear, along with my Tahoe,"

"I'm on it, Sugar. You heading out?"

"Already on the road. I'll be in touch when I can, Daddy. Thanks for the help." **Layne disconnected that call and made another,** "Sarge. It's Osterman. I could use some help."

"You found my phone number, Osterman, I'm sure you can find my place."

~

Layne spent two days in Philly doing reconnaissance on two EMTs who worked the Stacy Remington assassination. On the day of the hit, she made a call, "It's on." At 10 PM, she listened to 9-1-1 dispatch send the EMTs to a call. She plugged the address into her GPS and drove to the location. "Enjoy this call, guys, it's the last one of your lives." Within minutes, sirens and lights cut through the night. The ambulance was just gaining speed when it neared her. She set her sight on the driver, whispered "Geronimo," and took the shot. The ambulance swerved left-right-left, jumped the curb, traveled a few hundred feet, and crashed sideways into a tree. She waited for movement inside the driver's cab.

"He's dead." From the corner of her eye, she saw the back door of the ambulance swing open and an EMT hop out. He rounded the corner toward the driver's side, quickly realized he couldn't open that door, so he headed toward the passenger side. Layne whispered, "Geronimo," and took the shot. As she walked away, she whispered, "Shift's over."

~

The assassin parked her borrowed ride as close to the tree line on the tiny cul-de-sac as possible, then hoofed it to the sweet little cottage with a blue Honda parked on the driveway. Twenty-three-year old, Kelly Thompson, never knew what hit her when she exited her back door that morning. She was dead before the screen door slammed behind her. Layne pulled Kelly's body into the shrubs and headed inside. "Twelve minutes to change and get to Brothers' place. Tight, but doable." The assassin entered Kelly's perfectly cared for bedroom, opened a few drawers and took what she needed. "Medical pants and shirt." She tossed the jacket and wool cap she pulled off the dead chick onto the bed and got to work. She was changed and in the blue Honda within four minutes. "Right on schedule." She sang her little ditty along the way, "Find a Penny, shoot the fuck, all day long, you'll have good luck."

~

Penny was heading toward the stairs at the second-floor landing when she heard Kelly

Thompson's car coming down the street. The blue Honda was in desperate need of a muffler, and it announced itself long before it arrived at Ted's log cabin. Penny took a quick look out the window. "The Honda isn't parked where Kelly normally parks it." She eyed the woman walking to the front door. "That's not Kelly. Her walk is off. Her energy is off." Penny raced to the little area between Ted's office and den, unlatched the top of a hidden door, and snuck into the root cellar seconds before the doorbell rang and the front door opened. Penny didn't move from her perch on the top step.

The woman called out, "Hi Penny, it's Kelly." Silence. "Hey, Penny, did you forget about our session?" Silence.

Penny concentrated on the footfalls that moved from room to room on the first floor. She pulled and held a breath when her phone came to life in the distance. Mary Chapin Carpenter's *I Feel Lucky* filled the kitchen where she'd left her cell. In seconds, the song faded then after a moment of silence the tune began again. As soon as it stopped the house phone rang and a series of clicks put a big-ass relic of an answering machine to work. Penny strained to hear his voice coming from his office.

"Hey, Lucky. I'm with Fred. Call me back when you finish your session. We're bringing pizza."

The footfalls picked up speed, "So, you are here, Lucky. I will find you and finish you before pizza delivery."

Penny crouched as the assassin ran up to the second floor. She took that opportunity to move from the steps down into the root cellar. Doors slamming and furniture flipping covered the sounds of her breathing and banging heart. She counted the footfalls as they made their way to the first floor—and stopped on the other side of the hidden door.

The assassin's call chilled Penny to the bone, "I'll destroy this place looking for you. I've got an hour to kill before I kill you. I will prevail you bitch."

"I didn't prevail. I fucked up that mission, but I sure hit the mark on the senator—biggest hit I've ever done…"

"Moon River, wider than a mile..." The assassin parked the F-150 in thick brush across from the senator's home on the barrier island of Skidaway, Georgia. She'd been to her fire site several times, learned the lay of the land, and the habits of the senator. She checked her watch, "He'll be stepping out any minute, for a long, solitary look at the wakening river." She'd no sooner finished the sentence when the screen door squeaked open and he stepped out. "The senator is in residence." She set her sight, "The senator is in sight." She took a breath, exhaled it fully, and took the shot. "The senator is down." Before she'd moved completely away, the senator's wife rushed to the wrap-porch and fell to her knees.

Layne Osterman, contract killer for The Realm was on the main road by the time emergency response vehicles barrel-assed toward the senator's home. "Eli isn't going to like that it wasn't a clean kill shot, but even if Morgan survives, he won't be running for president, so the mission was a success." She smiled wide, patted the long gun resting between the two front seats, and finished her song. "Dream maker, you heart breaker."

Pleased with her overall success, Assassin Babe settles in for a longer than usual stretch of driving. "No more motels and overnights. I need to push through. I can rest when I get to Alaska—after I fuck the hell out of Eli, that is."

*What is your decision, Mrs. Ferraro?*


Felicity Ferraro pulls her burgundy Lexus into the underground parking garage of J. Edgar at 8 PM. On the way to the meeting she had second and third thoughts, turned around and headed for home, then turned back again, arriving later than she would have liked. She pulls into a space near the elevator, checks herself in the rearview mirror, and flips open the lock on the door. She takes the keys from the ignition just as the lights in the garage go out.

FICA Director, John Maxwell, steps from a dark corner, opens The Widow's door, reaches in and takes the keys from the stunned woman's hands. "Good evening, Mrs. Ferraro. Leave your purse in the car and please follow me." He takes her elbow, helps her out of the SUV, drops her keys onto the driver's seat, and closes the door behind her. He leads her to a black Escalade parked closest to the elevator, opens the passenger door, and settles her in. "We're going for a ride. If at any time you want out of this vehicle, all you need do is say so. Is that clear?"

"Yes."

"Mrs. Ferraro, are you voluntarily accompanying me?"

"Yes."

John exits the garage seconds before it is relighted. He checks his rearview mirror in time to see Agent Amanda Rhys drive Felicity's SUV onto Pennsylvania Avenue, park it, and leave it with the engine running. Seconds later a man walks by, opens the driver side door, and walks away. John keeps his eyes on the rearview and smirks when Mike falls in line five or so cars behind the Escalade. "Mrs. Ferraro, you took great risk dropping your note."

"It ended up in the right hands," she says flatly.

"It ended up in the hands of a Rocco Fiancetti operative."

The Widow pales, "I thought he was a Fed. He's RFI? Why did he turn the note over to you?"

"He didn't. Let's just say that the FBI and RFI are very plugged into one another and play nice, but both organizations want to get their hands on Felicity Ferraro and Mathis Reynolds, so we're not above cutthroat actions."

There is a bit more paling of her beautiful face, replaced quickly by an intense flushing, "You know about Mathis?"

"Of course we know. Let me give you a quick rundown of our investigation." John gives her what they know, plus whole lot of conjecture. "The Realm has gone dark; perhaps it has disbanded completely. Mathis Reynolds sits at the top of the organization, so any information you are willing to provide should be focused on him. We believe Turner Rodgers acted as conduit until stepping back to run for president. He was replaced by you. Your original role for the members of the organization was The Fixer. You protected clients from criminal prosecution and became overseer of the assassination squad for The Realm. The organizational structure of the criminal syndicate is an octopus, headed by The Body, and supported by eight appendages that we refer to as The Arms. We have identified two of those arms, Eli Reynolds and Jack McGovern. The six other people at the leadership level recently learned they'd been played by the head of the organization. We suspect they're pretty pissed and without anyone controlling them, we expect they'll be acting out against Realm members or reaching out to the Bureau for deals." John lets that settle before continuing. "We know more, but for the purposes of this evening, we're focusing on you and your motivations. Mathis Reynolds has your children, or he knows where your children are located, which is how he is keeping you under his control."

Felicity turns toward the passenger side window.

John straightens in his seat and checks the side- and rearview mirrors.

"Mrs. Ferraro, an urgent matter has come up."

She faces him again.

"Please keep your eyes forward or on me. Understood?"

"Yes."

"A vehicle has been following us since we pulled from J. Edgar. The occupants of that vehicle work for RFI. They have orders from Rocco Fiancetti to take you to his Compound, where you will stay until you tell him everything you know about The Realm, its leader, and its upper echelon members."

She begins shaking her head, "Rocco Fiancetti can't offer me immunity."

"No, but he can find your children. That is what you want?"

"Yes."

"Mrs. Ferraro, Mr. Fiancetti is very eager to find Mathis Reynolds. In doing so, he will find your children."

"Director Maxwell, everyone in law enforcement wants to find Mathis. What makes Mr. Fiancetti's motivation unique?"

"Retribution. He wants Mathis Reynolds to pay the ultimate price for killing Manuel Xavier. A father's grief is powerful motivation, and it is the only thing that drives Mr. Fiancetti."

"What about the FBI?"

"Full immunity is on the table regardless of who you work with. If you become an informant with the FBI, the Bureau will offer you protection, but it is in no way as secure as being at the Fiancetti Compound. I believe your husband proved that point when he killed Celia Brettenvue while she was under FBI guard."

The Widow's face heats again. "And if I don't talk to either the FBI or RFI?"

John is distracted by activity in his rearview; he sits a bit straighter in his seat and watches two cars cut ahead of Mike and get awfully close to his bumper. He quickly assess and plans. "Mrs. Ferraro, if you choose to go it alone, then I suspect you'll be talking to whomever is tailing us."

"You said RFI is tailing us."

"Yes, but there are two other vehicles as well. Tell me, Mrs. Ferraro, do you have any enemies?"

She tilts her head and raises a brow, "You can't be serious?"

"Has anyone threatened you within recent days?"

There is a pause before she starts cooperating. "Carter Thorndyke."

John smirks and gives his head a shake. "Mrs. Ferraro, when the former secretary of Homeland Security threatens your life, then you are nearing the end of it."

"I need to find my children first. I need to arrange their safety."

"What is your decision, Mrs. Ferraro?"

"RFI," she blurts.

John makes a quick U-turn followed immediately by Mike. They get through three sets of lights before the two other cars get out of the traffic commotion caused by John's sudden move. He cuts across and down several side streets, instructing The Widow as he drives, "When I pull to a stop, get out of this car and into the one that pulls beside us. Don't stop, just do it. Good luck, Mrs. Ferraro." John takes a corner and pulls to a stop in the middle of a street.

Mike pulls partly onto a curb and to the right of the Escalade. Penny pushes open the back door of Mike's vehicle, and Felicity jumps out of the FBI vehicle and into the RFI vehicle.

John lets Mike pull away then horizontally blocks the street with his SUV. He is standing outside the vehicle when one of the tails pulls behind him. He trains his weapon on the driver, "Don't fucking move." John raises his FBI shield overhead, and calls out to two DC Metropolitan officers who arrive on scene, "Cuff the men inside that vehicle. They, and the occupants of a tan SUV, partial tag 742 may have abducted a woman from a burgundy Lexus abandoned on Pennsylvania Avenue near the FBI headquarters. Officers, put out an APB on the tan vehicle and place these two under arrest. No one is to say a single word or ask a single question. This is an FBI case, officers."

John calls Director Shelby Webber, "Two men are being arrested by DC Metro. The arresting officers have been told the perps were involved in the abduction of a woman on

Pennsylvania Avenue. Other suspects are being sought in connection with the kidnapping. These individuals need to be squeezed by the long **Arm** of the law to ensure that our **homeland is secure**."

"Thank you, Director Maxwell. Have a pleasant evening."

Felicity Ferraro hasn't said a word since entering Mike's vehicle. Anxiety hits her full-on when the RFI jet is airborne. "This is a mistake. The other people following me tonight may be Mathis Reynolds' people. He'll know I talked to the FBI and that I'm with RFI. And if they aren't his people, then they're Carter Thorndyke's people, which means Turner Rodgers will find out and tell Mathis Reynolds that I was with John Maxwell. Oh My God! He'll kill my children. You need to take me back," she begins to hyperventilate, "please, take me back."

Her plea is met with silence.

"Director Maxwell said that all I had to do to end this was to ask to be let go."

Mike hands her a glass, "You aren't with the FBI anymore, Mrs. Ferraro. Drink this."

The beverage sloshes a bit in Felicity's shaky hand. Some dribbles down her fingers; still she sips enough to calm her in seconds and knock her out in minutes.

Penny leans toward Ted, "We just participated in a kidnapping, and now we're witnesses to a drugging. I think I need a sip of that Kool-Aid."

Ted smiles and whispers, "A sip? I want a whole fucking jug."

An RFI vehicle is waiting at Halifax Airport. Ted gets The Widow into the back seat with him. Mike and Penny sit up front. "It's an hour away so get comfortable. Mrs. Ferraro will be coming to anytime now."

Twenty minutes later, she wakes and immediately starts her conversation where she left off, "Really, you need to take me back." She looks at Ted and realizes she is no longer on the jet. She whirls directly into an F-3 hysterical tornado.

Mike addresses her from the front seat, "Mrs. Ferraro, we are very near our destination. When you arrive, Rocco Fiancetti will meet with you to discuss your options. Until then, please relax. My orders are to deliver you to The Compound, and that's what I intend on doing."

No other words are spoken until they arrive. Mike addresses Ted, "The building to your right is the Computer Center. Joy Fiancetti is waiting for you and Penny. Stay there until I come back to show you to your quarters." Mike steps from the Land Rover, opens the door for Mrs. Ferraro, and takes her elbow, "Rocco

Fiancetti is waiting for you in his office. This way, please."

Felicity's feet slip out from under her and she bangs awkwardly against her escort. Her clumsiness might be caused by the snow underfoot, or the aftereffects of a drugged drink, or simply her fraying nerves. It's most likely a combination of all three. She silently admonishes, *Pull yourself together. Lives depend upon this meeting.* She is totally in her headspace and completely unprepared for the likes of Rocco Fiancetti. "Wow."

He takes hold of her elbow and leads her inside, "Mrs. Ferraro, take a seat, please. I need a minute with Michael." The men head to the hallway, "On your way out of the Main Cottage, stop at the medical unit and remind Dr. Weinstock's team, and Manuel, that The Widow is in residence. Manuel is not to move freely without confirming her whereabouts. When I am done with her this evening, she will be brought to the Medical Center. Maura will give her a physical workup. Make sure you mention that The Widow arrived at our facility with a bandage on her hand, and forearm. Have Maura contact John to confirm she had the bandages when he retrieved her this evening. Assign Maura and Steve as onsite, overnight security. The Widow will be with me for a half-hour. I will accompany her to the Medical Center, so you may vamoose. Get Penny and Ted settled in their new quarters. Let Ted know he is on 24/7 guard duty beginning at 8 AM. Get some rest, Michael. You and Steve will be traveling within the next 24 to 36 to meet up with Fred."

"Leavy?"

"We are close." He taps Mike on the shoulder, "Good luck." He returns to his office. "Mrs. Ferraro, you and I will begin our work now. Please explain the injury to your hand and forearm."

"I had a disagreement with a wine glass. It won."

"How long ago?"

"January 21st. The day I learned The Realm was disbanded, and I was offered for consumption by the wolves."

"It appears the wolves were circling this evening. This is what has transpired during your travels. Reports of your kidnapping are being released to the press as we speak. John Maxwell has confirmed a kidnapping attempt was planned for this evening by Carter Thorndyke. Two men are in custody and will remain so; two others managed escape. The timing of the abduction attempt is fortuitous on several fronts. Mathis Reynolds will learn that you are missing. When he looks for a suspect, all signs will point to Thorndyke, and so for the time being he is unaware that RFI has you." Rocco studies her face, looking for a tell. He sees nothing but strain and dark circles. He does the whole hand over fist and twirling thumbs thing he does when he is in contemplation. "Tell me, Mrs. Ferraro, if Mr. Reynolds contacts

Turner Rodgers about your kidnapping, what will the senator say?"

"That he was in earshot when Thorndyke threatened me. If Turner's head is free of booze at the time of questioning, he'll repeat the threat."

Rocco smiles—wide. "And the threat issued by Thorndyke?"

Felicity shifts in her seat and smiles at her host. "I believe his words were, 'You're a spitfire, I'll give you that, Mrs. Ferraro, but mark my words, there will come a day when you find yourself at my mercy. Again, fair warning, I show no mercy. When I demand answers from you, you'd be wise to give me answers'."

"If that's the case, Mr. Reynolds has already begun a search."

She laughs heartily. "On this matter, Mr. Fiancetti, you are very wrong. Mathis is done with me. He told me so in no uncertain terms."

"Mathis Reynolds is neither done with you as an employee or as his sexual fix, Mrs. Ferraro. You are a beautiful, brilliant, strong, albeit evil woman. These are the things Mathis Reynolds finds irresistible."

The Widow's blue eyes frost. "I think you overestimate my importance to him, Mr. Fiancetti."

"I think you underestimate it, Mrs. Ferraro. The Body of The Realm plays only one type of game. The long game. He was married to and using Stacy Remington for a dozen years. When he determined her use was overshadowed by her threat against his organization, he had her killed. Reynolds has only begun playing with you. He is using your children as leverage so you will handle the fallout from his disbanding The Realm, but his real motivation is to use your children as leverage to get you and keep you for himself. So long as he thinks you have not turned against him and are still his for the taking, then your children are safe. I am quite sure his search for you has already begun, but it won't last long. I suspect we have two weeks tops."

Reality hits The Widow hard and fast. "Then my children have two weeks tops."

"Si, Mrs. Ferraro."

# Breaking News

Turner Rodgers is easing into his daily inebriation. While he pours a pint of gin, he makes a call. "Did you take Felicity Ferraro?"

"No. My men are in lockup, and last I checked she wasn't with them."

"Don't fucking play games, Carter. Two of your men are in lockup. John Maxwell said there were two others and they might have taken her."

"Who the fuck believes John Maxwell?"

"The people investigating Felicity's disappearance, but they're the least of your problems. For your sake, I hope The Body believes you."

Turner is on his third pre-noon gin when his private cell rings. The man who suddenly wishes he were passed out cold answers the call, "Didn't think I'd hear from you again."

"Where is she?"

"Don't know."

"Who has her?"

"Don't know that either."

"Don't fuck with me Turner. Did Thorndyke take her?"

"He says he didn't, but he threatened to. I heard him say he'd get answers from her about The Body one way or the other. The two goons arrested near the kidnapping scene swear they didn't take her, and they don't think the two other goons grabbed her."

"Has her place been searched?"

"I have people watching, and they haven't seen anyone go in or out, but there were hours between the actual kidnapping and when the press first identified Felicity by name. Entry to her place could have happened before news broke. If Thorndyke has her, then he's been inside her home. His singular mission is finding out who The Body is."

"He already knows. He laid out his theory to the Gang the other night after you and Felicity left the meeting. He's figured it out."

"If he knows who you are, then why go after Felicity?"

"He wants to know where I am."

"Does she know?"

"No."

"If he has her, she's dead or soon will be." Turner pulls a few long ones, then does the big ask. "Any chance she's with the Feds?"

"If she is, she's dead or soon will be."

Carter Thorndyke

There is absolutely no reason for him to make a trip into DC other than nostalgia. The former secretary of Homeland Security spends just over an hour in traffic on the round-trip. His cell phone begins chirping from the passenger seat of his Lincoln Aviator as he nears his estate. He ignores the calls, but counts each as he moves along a lovely two-lane road that winds through farmland and along the rolling hills of Great Falls, Virginia. The heavy-hearted man is surprised at the smile that creases his face, warmed by the feeling he gets here, only here. "Home," he sighs the word. The man with a plan parks his SUV where the gravel driveway meets the snow covered terrain. "Beautiful piece of real estate, even in the dead of winter." He closes his eyes and thinks back to a few months ago when the grass was green, the trees were full, and the duck pond was aflutter. "That's when this place is at its best."

Carter picks up his phone and scrolls through the list of missed calls. He laughs, "A virtual who's who of the power center of DC— that's what some will think when they see who burned up my phone today. Others will know these people as thugs and criminals. I think of them as my legacy. My final gift to the authorities. If the world learns about me, they learn about all of us." He thinks back to her threat…

"Save your threats, Carter. I know where every bone of criminality perpetrated by everyone in this room is buried. You'd be well advised to ignore the misguided belief that dead women don't talk. I assure you, should anything happen to me, your files will be in the hands of the FBI, DOJ, and RFI within 48-hours of my being reported missing. Come to think of it Carter, purely for shits and giggles, your set of incriminating documents will also be sent to the secretary of Homeland Security."

"Well, she's gone—so I'm fucked." The man steps outside his SUV, leans back, takes a long look around, and several deep breaths. "Really beautiful." When he's had his fill, he climbs back inside, then closes and locks the doors. He takes a final look at his phone and scrolls, "All formers. Every one of them used to be somebody, Secretary of Defense, Attorney General, White House Chief of Staff, Treasury Secretary, Appellate Court Judge, and let's not forget the man who thinks he will be the next president of the United States. Thank you all for calling this morning. I'm sure the Feds will be crawling up your asses before I'm buried six feet deep."

The man who used to be good and important puts his cell back onto the passenger side seat, opens the glove box, pulls out a loaded gun, swiftly puts it into his mouth and pulls the trigger. If he had waited another five seconds, he could have taken an incoming call and would have had the opportunity to speak with The Body, himself.

*Why, indeed?*

Joy, Annie, and Kitt are at the Computer Center. Again. They are working the topography angle. Again.

"Ladies, I need to work on something else for a while. Please continue your work on locating the Ferraro children. The urgency to produce findings is foremost now that The Widow is a guest at The Compound. Rocco thinks we have a window of about two weeks."

"Have you met Mrs. Ferraro, yet? I've heard she's gorgeous."

"No."

"Okay, so that topic of conversation is over. I guess it's back to analyzing sand, leaves, twigs, and water." Annie sips coffee from a soup-bowl sized mug as she keystrokes. With the touch of one of those keys, a wall-mounted 10' screen comes to life displaying the fourth video text Felicity Ferraro received from Mathis Reynolds, his voice now confirmed through analysis. Annie freeze-frames an image and smiles when she starts talking, "Kitt," the mother-daughter duo laugh at the reference.

"Still can't call me Mom?"

"Not when we're working. Don't know why it's a problem, I call John Maxwell 'Dad' while we work, but 'Mom' just isn't cutting it for me."

"Double standard."

"Yeup. Anyway, the video shows the lower extremities of Mathis Reynolds and the four Ferraro kids at a beach. When you review the images, ignore them completely this go around, concentrate on the topography only, the sand, both wet and dry, and the color of the sky and the ocean."

They watch in silence.

Annie claps her hands once, "Okay."

Kitt smiles. "Fred does that."

"Does what?"

"Claps his hands together when he starts talking through a case."

Annie shrugs. "Didn't know I clapped my hands." She shrugs again, "Okay, let's pull apart the video. The dry sand where Mathis is sitting is white."

"Pure white, like baby powder white," Kitt remarks.

Annie raises a brow.

"I spend my time with babies, so I know their powder, and that looks like baby powder. That sand is barely granular it's so soft."

"Mmm. And the water is blue, Littleton College blue."

"It's called azure."

Annie nods. "Let's do some research on what makes water appear blue or in this case azure." She keystrokes a bit then reads, "When sunlight hits the ocean, the water absorbs the long-wavelength colors of red, orange, yellow, and green. The remaining light is composed of the shorter wavelength of blues and violets. That's the color people see—it becomes the color of water. It's really a wonderful phenomenon. Can you imagine the ocean looking like water in a drinking glass?" Annie keystrokes a bit more then reads, "In shallow waters, light is able to penetrate all the way to the bottom, and the makeup of the ocean floor becomes a factor in determining water color."

Kitt goes off-topic for a minute. "Annie, what time of year was that video text sent to Felicity Ferraro?"

"Around the time of Senator Morgan's assassination, why?"

Kitt thinks a moment, "He was killed in mid-January, so we should be looking at warm winter places. No sense looking in Mayflower– Laurel Falls or anyplace like it. No one would be sunning and sanding in New England and the like in January."

Annie nods, does a bit more keystroking and a bit more reading, "Caribbean sand is white and the waters appear turquoise, right color sands, wrong color water. Hawaiian sand, depending on where you are on the islands, can be red, green, black, white, pepper, and golden brown, and the water is green-blue or varying shades of blue, wrong color sands across the board, a tossup on the water color. Did you know there were so many colors of sand?"

"No. Try Australia, Annie."

"Why?"

"Hunch."

"Australian beaches run the gamut in sand color ....... wait, there's a beach with blindingly white sand that looks like baby powder." She raises a brow and smirks. "Whitehaven Beach, on Whitsunday Island, Queensland." Annie does another search, "Whitehaven boasts the purest sand in the world at 98 percent pure silica. The four-mile-long beach is met at the shore by dazzling azure-colored water. Maybe Mathis Reynolds was in Queensland when he made the beach video text."

"Now what?" Kitt asks.

"We check real estate, and if we crap out, we look for more sandy white beaches and azure oceans."

"Be back! Turn on the news!" Joy hollers as she races from the Computer Center. Annie changes the overhead screen to a news station.

**Breaking News: Carter Thorndyke, Former Secretary of Homeland Security, dead of an apparent suicide...**

Rocco pokes his head into the Medical Center and whispers to Ted Brothers, who just started his 24/7 guard gig of The Widow, "Felicity Ferraro is not to leave this facility. Further, The Compound is on blackout status. No social media, no television, no news, nothing." Rocco has just exited the building when he and Joy literally bang into one another and unison, "You heard?"

"Si. Let's go." They meet up with Mike along the way, who's sporting a 'what the fuck' look on his barely awake face. "Ah, news is traveling swiftly. Master Michael, I instituted a total blacking of information for all facilities except the Computer Center. The Widow is not allowed wind of Carter Thorndyke's death."

"Do we know for sure it was a suicide?"

"Not yet, Michael. Let's talk inside the Center." Annie and Kitt stop their research and listen to their boss. "I expect John to advise when he can. He got in late last night from a visit to The Widow's home in Chevy Chase. His B&E and subsequent pilfering took place before announcements of the kidnapping were made. Now that The Widow is unreachable and The Realm is without illumination, communique options for The Body are limited. Reynolds probably contacted Turner Rodgers who might have fingered Carter Thorndyke for the abduction. That would have sent Reynolds on Thorndyke's trail, but—"

Kitt quietly opines, "Nope."

Rocco laughs, "Ah, a new country heard from. Please, continue your interruption."

"The sequence of events is nonsensical. They wouldn't pass muster in a mystery novel. Editors are like wardens—nothing gets past them—**this** certainly wouldn't. The bad guy abducts a woman who sits at the highest level of an international crime organization, and within hours the bad guy kills himself. There are too many missing pieces, like why did he kidnap her? He had to have had a reason. Did he want answers to questions? If so, why didn't he ask any questions? Did he want to send a message? If so, to whom? Did he want retribution? If so, for what? Regardless of motivation, Thorndyke didn't get anything for his efforts, hell he killed himself within hours of the abduction without doing **anything**. No way—there's absolutely no way the head of The Realm is going to think Thorndyke took Felicity, not long-term anyway."

"Is there more opining, oh Writing One?"

"A question. Why did Thorndyke kill himself?"

"Why, indeed?"

*Off the grid – but getting closer.*

Fred has been snowmobiling for the better part of two days and hasn't made a dent in the expanse. He spent the first day tooling around Kenai Lake, stopping from time to time to walk trails, particularly those with nearby cabins. He saw footprints, but received no call-outs about his trespassing. He spent the second day following trails along Skilak Lake before hanging at a dock, looking through binoculars, and working through a nudge that pressed deep. "I feel you, Leavy. Hang on. I'm bringing you home this time." His mind wanders, not to when she was taken from under his watch, but to when they were reunited…

Fred entered the great room at the Fiancetti Compound for the first time. Everything faded away when he saw the woman he searched for night and day, the woman he concerned over every second of every minute for months on end. "Leavy." He opened his arms, and when he had her tight in his fold, he kissed the side of her head. "Few others have healed my fractured heart the way you are doing right now," the man choked.

Leavy managed a single word before crumbling in his arms. "Fred."

"I searched. I would have searched until my dying day."

"I know. Every time you came to the farmhouse, I wanted to come out of hiding and tell you. I'm sorry for the worry I put you through."

"All water, now." He wiped her tears and pulled her in for another hug. When he pulled himself together, he walked away.

"Not walking away this time." It's day three, and Fred Serpico is back at Skilak to see if the nudge he had was a one off—it wasn't. He walks the length of the dock he was on the day before, locks his sight on the north side of the lake, and lets his attention fix on his connection to Leavy. He pulls a small notebook from his pocket and draws the outline of the lake, then marks an X wherever there is smoke rising from chimneys, or where he sees the pitch of a roof in the distance, or docks that jut out onto the lake—anything that shows signs of life is marked in his book, which he nearly drops when a voice comes from behind him.

"You're on my land."

Fred whips around, fully expecting to find a rifle trained on him, "No harm intended. I got swept up in the beauty of this spot yesterday and was called back."

"I saw you yesterday. Didn't bother me then, bothers me now."

Fred approaches with his hand outstretched, "Fred Serpico, I'm sorry to have disturbed you."

"Serpico, like the cop in that movie?"

Fred laughs, "Not quite."

"But you're a cop?"

Fred gets a feeling from this guy, a good feeling, "A detective."

"You looking for someone?"

"A woman."

"Ain't we all," the grizzly man of about fifty smiles. "She your woman?"

"My partner."

The man pulls his hand down his long brown beard, "Tough place to be missing. You think she's holed up in a cabin?"

Fred nods and looks out over the lake again, "Not by choice."

"You think she's on the north side?"

"Just a feeling. I got it yesterday, and it's stronger today."

The man steps toward Fred and extends his hand, "Name's Wooly Jones. I know every damn inch of this lake. Lower and Higher Skilak campgrounds are on the north side, and there are a handful of small out-camps, but they're mostly closed this time of year. Unless your partner's inside a cabin, and she stays there, she's not gonna survive long." He does another pull of his beard before continuing, "Set between and behind the campgrounds, there are a dozen or so trapper-style cabins where she could take shelter, but they're bare bones as far as amenities. This time of year, only experienced campers and ice fishers spend time there. If your partner is on the northside, your best bet is the handful of larger homestyle cabins, mostly taken out as long rentals. Folks in those cabins don't like to be bothered, though. Still, they might have seen something in the area, so it's worth a talk to."

Fred asks Wooly straight on, "Any chance you'd help with a search party. My team arrives tomorrow, and we want to get out within a day or two?"

"Could help, but if you're all moving in on snowmobiles, you need authorized permission from the refuge manager. That area on the north side is Kenai National Wildlife Refuge."

"Any chance you know where I can find the manager?"

The man extends his hand again, "Name's Wooly Jones, Skilak Lake Refuge Manager."

Fred shakes the man's hand and laughs big, but not nearly as big as Wooly Jones.

*In a nutshell — a big-ass nutshell.*

Rocco is readying for his third RFI/FBI video conference with Felicity Ferraro. It was slow going initially, but once she began providing information, she's been forthcoming, enough that full immunity is on the table. It is far from a sure thing, however. The men expect a new round of reticence when the snitch learns John went into her home, cracked her safe, and has in his possession the files she assembled on some of the most plugged in members of DC power and society.

The head of RFI answers John's call. "You're on with Rocco Fiancetti and Felicity Ferraro. Please identify yourselves."

"John Maxwell, Director of FICA."

"Shelby Webber, Director of the Federal Bureau of Investigation. Mrs. Ferraro, I will be a spectator to this conference call. Do you understand?"

"Yes."

"Do you consent?"

"Yes."

"Without courtesy of Miranda?"

"Yes."

"Very well, please proceed, Director Maxwell."

"Mrs. Ferraro, I have in my possession eight files, each one held inside an expandable brown folder commonly used by lawyers. I also have five files banded together by elastic and enclosed inside a similar expandable—"

The Widow gasps, "You have—"

"Everything. We have everything, Mrs. Ferraro. We no longer need you to make a case against the Gang of Eight, as you referred to them in countless documents, so this is how this will work. Every question raised by the law enforcement individuals present today will be answered by you. The first indication that you are unwilling to cooperate, are less than forthcoming with information, or deceitful in any way, immunity is off the table. Is that understood, Mrs. Ferraro?"

She nods.

"Please state your understanding."

"I understand the rules, Director Maxwell."

"Very good. Rocco, please proceed."

"Explain the files."

"The Realm is framed as an octopus. The Body is Mathis Reynolds. The appendages make up a leadership group called the Gang of Eight. Director Maxwell mentioned your organization refers to the appendages as The Arms which is an apt description as their functions are far-reaching." She squirms and draws a full breath, "I should provide some background. I'll begin with Turner Rodgers and

Eli Reynolds. Until recently, the Gang thought Turner was The Body, the head of the organization, the person to whom they pledged allegiance, the one who devised The Plan—"

"Explain."

"I'm afraid I can't, Mr. Fiancetti. I'm not sure if anyone other than Mathis knows what The Plan entails, but we all know it involves getting the world's top ranked cyber huntresses into The Realm's possession. As for Eli, the Gang thought Turner brought him onto the leadership level because of their longstanding association."

"Please confirm or deny RFI's investigative findings on the senator and the younger Reynolds brother. The two met in 1999 when Turner was a congressman and Eli was an intern on Capitol Hill. They maintained an association, and Eli most likely introduced Turner to Mathis."

"That's my understanding, I don't know what the others in leadership thought, but I assumed Eli was muscle for Turner. It is obvious now that he was a spy for Mathis, the person listening and reporting back whether Turner conveyed Mathis' plans accurately, and whether the Gang members stayed in line." She runs her fingers across her brow, "Have you a tissue, Mr. Fiancetti? It's a bit warm in here."

Rocco hands her a starched white handkerchief and a bottled water, "When you're ready, Mrs. Ferraro, please continue with your assessment."

She pulls another long breath, "The Gang of Eight: Carter Thorndyke, Thomas Haley, Eugene Jackson, Christie Sargent, Stephanie Butler, Robert Cantor, Jack McGovern, and Eli Reynolds."

John seeks additional confirmation, "Mrs. Ferraro, please confirm or correct after each name and title is repeated back to you." Shelby, and Rocco begin writing when John begins speaking. "The leadership members of The Realm, the ones identified by you as members of the Gang of Eight, a subsidiary of the criminal enterprise headed by Mathis Reynolds, aka The Body, are: former secretary of Homeland Security, Carter Thorndyke."

"Yes."

"Former attorney general, Thomas Haley."

"Yes."

"Former secretary of defense, Eugene Jackson."

"Yes."

"Former White House chief of staff, Christie Sargent."

"Yes."

"Former secretary of treasury, Stephanie Butler."

"Yes."

"Former Appellate Court judge, Robert Cantor."

"Yes."

"Former deputy director of the FBI, Jack McGovern."

"Yes."

"Former Army ranger, Eli Reynolds."

"Yes."

"Please continue."

"The files retrieved from my home safe are for the following individuals: Rodgers, Thorndyke, Haley, Jackson, Sargent, Butler, Cantor, and McGovern. The banded files are for the following individuals: Roland Gaffney, Benton Brettenvue, Dominique Brettenvue, Celia Brettenvue, and Dan Shea."

"Are there files on the Tango project leaders?" John asks.

"I would think Turner Rodgers has those files. He worked with Benton Brettenvue and Antonio Alvarez on Tango, a return on investment project linked to a change in legislation overseen by the U.S. Treasury and Energy departments that would allow private investors into the LNG import and export business. I don't know the particulars other than the leaders of Tango came from countries that had LNG imports or exports nearing the end of restrictive contracts with IOCs. Aside from Antonio Alvarez, the men of Tango had no participation in the Realm organization."

"Was Antonia Alvarez part of the Gang of Eight at any time?"

"Not to my knowledge, but his involvement with the organization preceded my active participation."

"Is there a file on Mathis Reynolds?" John asks.

"I don't have one. I didn't know Mathis had anything to do with The Realm until very recently. Again, Turner Rodgers might have a file. He, Roland Gaffney, Eli Reynolds, and Paul Ferraro were the only people who knew about Mathis being The Body, to my knowledge. It wasn't until Paul's arrest that I learned how involved he was at the upper echelon. He was the individual who identified Mathis Reynolds as being The Body."

"Proceed with the inventory from the Ferraro safe, Director Maxwell," Shelby pushes in.

"There is a zipped container with a dozen or so flash drives and there are three financial ledgers. Please explain, Mrs. Ferraro."

"The flash drives contain every piece of correspondence or legal filings or research I did on the Gang of Eight. There is also information on named enemies of The Realm or Turner Rodgers. That's where you will find information on Abigail Forrester and Penny Meehan, among others. The flash drives also have information on the contract killings done by Paul Ferraro and Mason Trellis. As for the ledgers, one documents payments I received from the Gang of Eight for my services as The Fixer, one documents payments Preston and Porter received from other DC players who found themselves in need of a fixer, and the final one documents debits and credits for the contract killings I facilitated."

Shelby pushes in again "Proceed with the inventory, Director Maxwell."

"Aside from the things already itemized, Mrs. Ferraro, there were personal papers, jewelry, and other standard fare for bedroom safes. And there was a note."

"Read the note, Director Maxwell."

"Don't ever become my enemy."


Felicity becomes unhinged. She shoots from her seat, bolts toward the door, is blocked from leaving by Ted Brothers, which ratchets her into an immediate hyperventilating frenzy. Rocco and Ted try to wrangle her in, as her screams resound, "My kids, my kids, he's going to kill my kids. I shouldn't have come. He knows! He knows! He knows everything!"

FBI Agent, Candace Hayes responds to the commotion and administers a sedative. Within seconds Felicity Ferraro is out cold and being moved to the medical suite.

# ALASKA

Layne Osterman made really good time getting to Kenai—that won't be the case in her getting to the cabin. "Snow is piling fast. Traveling the access road will be tough going. If I get stuck on that road, I'm fucked." Her Tahoe fishtails; she corrects it. "Slow it down. Handle the roads. Watch for tagalongs. If the coast is clear, get as close as you can then head in on foot." She leaves her Chevy Tahoe on a snowy pull off on Lake Road, a mile or more from the log cabin. She's trudging through and making good time; still, she picks up the pace as nightfall fills the woods around her. When she's 200 yards from the safe house, she calls out to Eli, "Ranger, it's Osterman." She's about to call out again when the cabin door is practically pushed from its hinges.

"What the fuck are you doing here, Layne?"

"I need a place to lay low. I'm being hunted hard after the last mission. Can I come in; it's brick and snowy as fuck out here?"

Eli nods, and reluctantly steps aside. "One night, Layne, then you have to leave."

She begins to ask why, then sees the reason sitting on a couch by the fire. Some sort of emotion pinches deep until she sees the set of chains on the woman's ankle and a bandage on the back of her head.

"Who's your friend, Eli?"

"No friend, she's a job. That's why you can't stay, Layne. What about Wyoming, Montana, or Pennsylvania?" he refers to ranger veterans Blake Firestone, Chester Buckman, and Adam Noone.

"Can't go near them, especially not Noone. RFI is—"

Eli grabs hold of the sniper's bicep and squeezes.

She pulls free, "What the fuck, Eli?"

Layne follows his eyes toward the woman on the couch. Recognition dawns that the woman is Hannah Leavy, RFI cyber huntress. Recognition also dawns that the tail that's been on her for weeks isn't only after her because of the assassination of Curtis Morgan, but also because he wants his RFI partner back. And lastly, recognition dawns that she might have led RFI to the safe house. She decides to keep her mouth shut about that set of circumstances and get the hell out of Kenai at sunup.

Leavy hasn't been to her loft in days, and even though she suffers from headaches and bouts of dizziness, she asks permission to head up.

Eli unchains his prisoner, gets her settled, rechains her, and heads back to Layne. "Kitchen, now. Tell me about RFI."

She cautions herself. *Keep it cool. Keep it short. And lie your ass off.* "They have me for the two EMT shootings, the physical therapist neck break, and the job on Penny Meehan. I stayed low with Sergeant Noone at Blue Marsh Lake after those hits and before the Curtis Morgan assassination. I was heading back to Noone's place for some down time, but he diverted me, said he didn't want me settling back with him. I've been on the road since."

"Fuck, Layne, you've got the whole fucking world of law enforcement looking for you, so you came here?"

"First, I'm not stupid, Eli. No one is following me. I've been alone on the roads since Georgia. I didn't know you'd be here. I didn't know you were working a job. I had no other place to go. And I'm out of here as soon as the access road is plowed. How long do think it will take?"

"Plows won't come out until the snow stops. We'll know the access road is cleared when the recreational snowmobilers start riding the field, or my provisions guy makes it to the cabin. He's serious about not leaving his customers stranded, and since I need food and firewood, he'll show and we'll know. When the delivery comes, you go."

*One point nine two million acres.*

The RFI jet lands in near blizzard conditions at Ted Stevens International Airport in Anchorage—or more accurately, the RFI jet slides to a landing in near blizzard conditions. According to the group's travel guide, Mike, "The airport prides itself on never closing due to weather conditions and considers snow management business as usual." That should in no way suggest that landing a jet in whiteout conditions is business as usual.

Three RFI men stumble into an airport hangar, slapping one another's shoulders as though they'd beaten death's pull. "Shit, I was hoping there was an on-site wet bar in here. I need a few belts," Steve laments.

"Are you doing the driving?" the doctor asks.

"Nope, the recon specialist does the driving. Why?"

Weinstock opens his carryon and hands off a couple nips, "Hope you like Tequila."

"Fuck man, right about now I'd drink rubbing alcohol."

"And I'd be onsite to declare you dead. Drink these instead."

The guys load themselves and their gear into a rental and begin their 150-mile trek to

Kenai Peninsula. The trip should take three hours—it takes seven. They find the motel Fred suggested not too far from Sterling Highway marker 58. The new arrivals check in, then head to a conference room where they meet Fred, who introduces a grizzly guy to the team. "That's Steve Phelps, RFI sniper and security analyst. That's Mike Monopoli, RFI ground and surveillance specialist. And that's FBI Special Agent, Gregory Weinstock. Men, this is Wooly Jones, refuge manager of Skilak Lake. I bumped into him when I was riding the trails."

Mike and Steve share a look and a laugh, "How big is the lake?" Mike asks Wooly.

"Fifteen miles long, and in certain parts, four miles wide," he smiles like a proud papa.

"And the land around it? How many acres we talking about?"

"Skilak Lake is part of the Kenai National Wildlife Refuge, and that section alone is 1.92 million acres."

The RFI men crack up, "And Fred just happened to run into the refuge manager while aimlessly wandering 1.92 million acres."

Wooly gets the joke, "He does this sort of thing a lot?"

"He does this sort of thing all of the time," Mike laughs. "He falls on top of, runs into, bumps up against, and just happens upon whatever or whoever he needs to get the job done."

"Good thing," Wooly says, "because we're looking for a needle in a 1.92 million acre, snow-covered haystack, **if** your team member is being held in that location. Your lead sure thinks she is."

"I say we take a look," Fred gives his hands a clap, then gives the marching orders. "We're here on a rescue mission. We want to bring Hannah Leavy home, but let's not forget that Senator Curtis Morgan's assassin is headed this way. She may already be here. Let's be on the lookout for her brand spanking new gray Chevy Tahoe." He hands his laptop to Mike, "Get Randy on visual."

The hipster dude is introduced to the grizzly dude and the two get to work. "What do you need, Wooly?"

"Aerials for these coordinates." Wooly keys some shit.

Randy keys some shit, and puts up a wide shot aerial view.

The men move close to the screen. Wooly and Randy start their back and forth. "Randy, zoom to the land north of the lake, now zoom in to the northwest corner, that's Lower Skilak Campground. Zoom in a bit more and you'll see a handful of trapper camps and two good-size homestyle cabins. Now, if you zoom back out and go east a bit, but before the big land dip toward the lake, that's Upper Skilak Campground. That's where the other trapper camps are. And if you zoom in further, you will see a cluster of trees that separate land clearings where three of the nicer, more sizeable homestyle cabins are located."

Fred pushes in, "Randy send that information to Mike's and Steve's cells."

"Will do, Tonto."

Fred growls.

Randy laughs, "You sound like 77. Speaking of which, his return to 275 is imminent. Have you been updating him?"

"Not yet."

"Got it."

Wooly pushes in, "By and by Fred, I talked to Fletch Faulkner last night. He runs a provisions delivery service to the cabins. People who rent long-term place orders and schedule deliveries that he takes deep by snowmobile. I asked Fletch about the cabin renters, specifically about women, he says two of the cabins have women. He hasn't seen either of them on his deliveries, but the provisions he's brought in have included period products, you know stuff women use."

Fred laughs his next question, "Did he tell you where these menstruating women are staying?"

"Cabin 4 and 5. He's making a delivery to Cabin 5 tomorrow if the access road is cleared."

Fred slaps Wooly on the shoulder, "You mean one of us is making the delivery."

"Suppose that's right Fred. Let me show you where. Randy, zoom deep near Upper Skilak." Wooly points to two cabins. "Here and here—these two cabins are separated by a mile of trees. The access road you see here is Lake Road. We'll have to travel in by truck to about here, then access the cabins by snowmobile. The land between the tree line and the cabins are free range, which means it's open to roamers and snowmobilers from 7 AM to 7 PM. The renters are used to some activity which bodes good for us. Making a surprise attack, though, isn't an option, so make a plan around a provision drop. Last thing, we can't go in until the access road is cleared, that also means no one can get out of those cabins 'til then either."

*The Widow Needs To Go Back.*


Joy was up all night listening to the voice recording John made during his drive around DC with Felicity Ferraro and watching the teleconference from the night before. She is fixated on two things when Rocco comes looking for her, "Listen to this exchange..."

"And if I don't talk to either the FBI or RFI?"

"Mrs. Ferraro, if you choose to go it alone, then I suspect you'll be talking to whomever is tailing us."

"You said RFI is tailing us."

"Yes, but there are two other vehicles as well. Tell me, Mrs. Ferraro, do you have any enemies?"

"You can't be serious?"

"Has anyone threatened you within recent days?"

"Carter Thorndyke."

"Mrs. Ferraro, when the former secretary of Homeland Security threatens your life, then you are nearing the end of it."

"I need to find my children first. I need to arrange their safety."

"What is your decision, Mrs. Ferraro?"

"RFI," she blurted.


"Interesting, mi amore."

"Thought you'd think so. Now, turn around."

"Should I lock the door?" he winks.

"No, you should open it and go back through it. Then you should go wake The Widow, slap her if need be, and have her tell you what caused Carter Thorndyke to issue a threat against her."

"I'd rather lock the door and turn you around."

"Go."

"Si."

"And record the conversation."

"Si."

Joy is waiting at the door for his return, her hand extended, "Phone, please."

"Gia, in the future choose a different side of the bed to crawl out of."

"I've not been to bed yet."

"Ah, that mystery is solved."

Joy ignores, presses play and hears Rocco's voice, "Good morning, Mrs. Ferraro." Joy stops the recording, "Please refrain from speaking for the next few minutes. One of you is all I can stand at the moment."

"Si, mi amore."

Joy starts the recording again, "Good morning, Mrs. Ferraro."

"Is it?" she croaked.

"Ah, I'm finding the jury is out on that."

Joy chuckles. "Shhhhh."

"You are the disrupting one, Gia."

"Shhhhh."

"I require information, Mrs. Ferraro."

"Shouldn't you be searching for my children, Mr. Fiancetti?"

"Si, but there have been developments that dictate our next moves."

"What information do you need?"

"Explain the threat made by Carter Thorndyke."

"The Gang was none too pleased when they learned Turner had deceived them about being The Body. He appeased most with offers of cabinet positions in his administration. The next morning, Malcolm Price declared his candidacy for president. Carter flipped a nut on me when he realized his power on the worldwide stage and on the national stage were gone. He assumed, rightly so, that Turner would lose against Mr. Price. Carter insisted I identify The Body and threatened to put my head on a spike when I refused."

"Your response to his threat?"

"I reminded him that before I was named conduit, I was The Fixer and I knew where every bone of criminality was buried. I let him and the others know that the files I built on each Gang member would be delivered to the FBI, DOJ, and RFI within 48-hours of my being reported missing or found dead. Then I told Carter I would arrange his file be sent to Homeland Security just for shits and giggles."

Joy starts the recording again, listens attentively, and declares, "The Widow needs to go back."

# Lewisburg, Pennsylvania

Mr. and Mrs. Mayor step off the privacy elevator into a silent penthouse apartment. The ping of the elevator and tiny yelp of their bundle of pink softly announce their arrival. Tiny dust particles take flight in the morning light, a silent reminder that the home has been alone far too long. Malcolm escorts mother and child to the master bedroom without word, kisses each on the top of their heads, and continues toward his office.

Gretchen nurses Baby Girl, gets her settled in the bassinet, quickly changes into comfy clothes, then sets about getting her man's head on straight. She starts by texting Randy.

**From Gretchen: Are you at 275?**
**From Randy: The Kid and The Justice are five minutes away.**
**From Gretchen: Come up privacy elevator. Baby Girl is sleeping in the master. Please keep an ear on her. I'll be with Malcolm in his office. Thank you.**
**From Randy: And if we wake Baby Girl to play with her?**
**From Gretchen: You wake it --- you own it.**

Gretchen waits, and when she hears the privacy elevator being called to the garage, she makes her way to Malcolm's office. The wife finds the husband in his customary pose, back pressed against a wall, his feet crossed at the ankles. He smiles when he sees her, although his smile doesn't go anywhere close to finding his eyes.

She crosses the room.

He doesn't move.

"Malcolm, I need you to hold me. I need the comfort of your arms, and I need to know you will come back to me," her eyes fill with tears that desperately need to fall.

Malcolm pushes from the wall and pulls Gretchen into his arms, "Woman." He holds her for a minute, then holds her at arm's length, places his hands onto her cheeks and stares. He just stares. "Woman," his word is carried on a breath of angst. He traces his thumb along stress creases and dark circles beneath her eyes, "Woman. I'm sorry I haven't been there for you, but I didn't leave you," he says with marked pain. "I will never leave you, Gretchen." He wraps his arms tight again and takes the tears she's held for weeks. The stressful and emotional turmoil of DelRae's birth, Curtis' death and funeral—all of the suppressed emotions pour from her and leave her physically incapable of moving. Malcolm lifts his wife, carries her to bed, and tucks her in for a nap near their slumbering daughter. He stands over his girls, rights himself in body and mind, then heads to the kitchen. Randy and Peyton bounce from the leather couch as he moves through, unsure what to say or do.

Malcolm motions for them to follow, "I'm glad you're here." They smile, but wait. "There's work to do on the campaign. Randy, you've probably got your hands full with RFI stuff, but if time allows, I'd like your help. And Peyton, the Malcolm Price presidential campaign most definitely needs you." After scrambling a few eggs and making a pot of coffee, he tries to distance himself from his father's death by reconnecting with his own life, "Any news on Leavy?"

"Nothing for sure, but some things are in the works."

"Good."

# FINDING LEAVY

Wooly Jones takes a call, exchanges a few words, and disconnects. "Fred, Lake Road is plowed. We can move in by truck, unload our snowmobiles and head deep. Two things to discuss. Fletch Faulkner will meet us to transfer the provisions, and he said there's a vehicle parked to the side of the access road a mile due south of the cabin we're heading to. Might be there's more than two people inside Cabin 5 now. Changes things, Fred."

The lead RFI member doesn't comment, he does what he always does, what he **needs** to do to process—he heads to an oversized window, crosses his arms, spreads his legs, locks his knees, and gets to it. After a bit, Fred begins. "If the vehicle is a Tahoe, then Layne Osterman, the assassin of Senator Curtis Morgan is at the cabin."

"Like I said, this changes things, Fred."

It's many minutes before Detective Serpico speaks again, "Wooly, any idea what the provisions are?"

"Usual load: food, waters, paper supplies, and firewood—there's always some firewood brought in."

Fred claps his hands once, "Okay, two man plan. Wooly, you'll be traveling in to make the provisions delivery. Steve you'll be perched for communications and a kill-shot." Fred waits for comment from either man. He receives none. "Wooly, you're gonna go in with the provisions, but you'll leave the firewood behind. We'll play the odds that the folks in Cabin 5 will need it and take you up on your offer to go back to the road to get it. This is your first delivery—and you're making it because Fletch got injured plowing, so the oversight shouldn't raise suspicions. While you're at the cabin get a lay of the land. If your first trip in turns to a shitshow, concentrate on Osterman and take her out if need be. Any questions?"

"Nope."

"Okay, Steve. You'll ride in with Wooly until you're just shy of the tree line, then perch yourself. You're gonna be the team's eyes and ears. I want to know every breath Eli Reynolds, Layne Osterman, and Hannah Leavy take. At the first sign of trouble, take out Reynolds. I'll be in the trees at the halfway point, Mike and Weinstock will stay on the access road in case the assassin isn't at the cabin or she somehow gets past us. At the first sound of a shot, you two move in. Okay, Mike, get everyone communications ready. Wooly, you're out of the loop."

"I know the drill, Fred."

"Okay boys, let's roll." Fred steps to the side and texts Randy.

**From Fred: Find out who Wooly Jones is.**

Leavy has been in the loft for hours. She's hungry, she's thirsty, and she needs to pee, but she is desperate to keep her distance from Eli. She heard Layne mention the date—February 14—and that she'd be leaving the cabin as soon as the access road was cleared. "Valentine's Day." Leavy's eyes sting with tears. "Eli will surely wine, dine, seduce, and rape me again." The captive lifts her listless eyes from a book she's pretending to read to stare outside. "It's really beautiful here. A perfectly beautiful place to die," she whispers wistfully.

"Did you say something?" Eli startles her from the top of the stairs.

"I just remarked how beautiful it is here, especially after yesterday's snow storm."

He takes a look out the window. "It is beautiful. May I sit with you for a minute, Leavy?"

She swings her legs from the window seat to make room.

"Provisions will be delivered sometime today. Layne will be leaving as soon as that happens. It's Valentine's Day. You and I will be spending time together. I've adjusted myself after your injury. I should not have hurt you, and I don't want to again," he reaches toward her and fingers a long ringlet that has fallen from her freaky bun.

Leavy wants to pull away. She doesn't dare.

This pleases her captor, her tormentor, her rapist. "Come downstairs, freshen up, and then you can come back here while I discuss a few things with Layne." He hands her the key, waits at the stairs, then walks her to the bathroom.

Leavy runs the water in the shower, but doesn't enter. She stands and stares at herself in the mirror. "I've changed. I look old. Minimal physical activity, lack of fresh air and sunshine, and a broken heart will do that to a person, I suppose." She has a good cry for herself, runs her head under the faucet so it looks like she washed her hair in the shower, and makes a promise. "The very first chance I get to escape, I'm taking it. I don't care if he shoots me. In fact, I hope he does."

Wooly drives the truck in and informs his riders along the way, "That trapper shack on the right is about a half-mile from where we're stopping. If this goes bad, or if there are injuries, take refuge there. Fletch will be nearby watching in case emergency exit is needed. Otherwise, we'll get you on the way out." He points to his right a bit farther up the road, "Steve, we'll be going in here. I'll take you to where you need to be. When I stop the snowmobile, get off quickly and walk until you see a dilapidated lean-to. Look to the right and you'll see a tree with a perfectly straight horizontal branch that makes the tree look like a cross. You'll know it when you see it. It's an easy climb and it has a platform perch. You'll be able to see straight through Cabin 5."

The truck stops, the men meet up with Fletch Faulkner and busy themselves loading Wooly's snowmobile. They barely see Layne's Tahoe pulled off to the side of the road, and no one goes anywhere near it.

Fred approaches Wooly, "You all set?"

"Yep."

Fred offers Wooly a firearm, knowing full well the man is already packing, "Here."

The grizzly bear of a man shakes his head. "You hang onto that, Fred, I've got Bessy with me."

Fred slaps Wooly's shoulder, "Bessy ever let you down?"

"Nope, she's the only woman who hasn't."

Fred laughs. "Good luck."

"Thanks, Fred."

Fred slaps Steve's shoulder, "Good luck, partner." As soon as they're seated and moving on the mobile, Fred receives a text:

**From Randy: Wooldruff Jones, ex-CIA.**

Fred laughs big, "Refuge manager my ass. He's a friend of Rocco Fiancetti's." The detective suddenly feels a whole lot better about the plan and their odds.

Leavy is escorted back to the loft and chained in.

"Do you need a book or something? You'll be up here for a while."

"I've got one, but I think I'll just daydream for a while."

Eli brushes her damp hair away from her face, "I'm glad you're beginning to like it here. Things will be different when Layne leaves." He bends and kisses the top of her head, then takes a look outside the window. "Snowmobilers are moving in the distance. The access road must be clear. You'll be able to see the provisions guy heading in. Let me know when, so Layne can get her gear on and hit the road."

Leavy swings her legs onto the window seat, the heavy chain pulling tight until she adjusts it. She leans her arm on the sill and rests her head on the crook of her elbow. In minutes she is lost in thought.

*Manuel, I'm sorry. I just can't do this anymore.*
*I wish I could suffer through until you find me, but—*

A quick flash of light comes from a section of trees where the wide expanse of open space meets heavy woods. She trains her eyes on the spot, careful not to draw the attention of Eli and Layne who are moving about the cabin. Leavy's heart thumps when she sees a second flash. She picks up her book and pretends she's engrossed.

"All set?" Eli asks from the stairs.

Leavy feigns surprise, "I'm sorry, did you say something?"

"I asked if you were all set."

She waves the book, "I guess I was caught up in this."

He smiles. He leaves.

Steve is set on the 'cross tree' perch and is scoping the cabin, "I see Leavy. She's on the second floor, looking out the window, kinda of daydreaming. I think she saw a flash when I set because she moved her head in my direction and is staring my way. The cabin is 1200 hundred yards from the tree line. The door on this side of the cabin opens in. A good portion of the first floor is windows. Just off of the entrance to the right is a room with couches and a fireplace. Leavy is above that room in an open loft. I think the kitchen is on the back left side of the house opposite the entrance door. Don't see any other occupants."

Leavy hears the snowmobile before she sees it. She sits up from her daydream position and surveys her surroundings.

Steve updates his team. "Leavy is sitting up. She's staring at the tree line. She probably hears the snowmobile. She's sees Wooly, and she's saying something. Eli Reynolds and Layne Osterman just entered the room below Leavy. They are putting on coats and boots. I doubt Wooly is gonna get inside."

Leavy watches Eli and Layne get ready. He looks up at her, "Don't fucking move or call attention to yourself. Layne and I will handle the provisions, so don't get any ideas. Understand?"

The gun in his hand makes everything perfectly clear. "Yes, Eli."

Steve updates his team, "Eli and Leavy just exchanged words. He was holding a gun in his hand, and issuing an obvious threat. The gun is in his righthand coat pocket. He just opened the front door. Wooly is nearing the cabin. Eli is outside and approaching the snowmobile. He has his hand on his gun in his pocket."

Wooly addresses Eli. "Cabin 5. I've got a provisions delivery."

"Where's Fletch?"

"Got hurt plowing Lake Road this morning. Asked me to run this stuff. Want to give me a hand."

"We can handle it," Eli motions to Layne and hands off a couple duffle bags. Eli takes the rest, "Wait here while we empty these."

Wooly doesn't look around; he's already seen enough.

Eli returns, hands off the empty duffles, "Where's the firewood?"

"Shit. I forgot it back at Fletch's truck. Sorry, man. This is my first run."

"I need it, today."

"Sure. Sure. I'll get it and bring it in." Wooly reaches to start his engine.

"Wait," Eli says. "Can you give my friend a ride to her vehicle?"

"Where's her vehicle?"

"Lake Road."

"Didn't see no car on the road. Probably buried." Wooly pulls his beard, "I can give her a lift—hop on."

Eli stops Layne, pulls her into a tight hug, and snarls, "Don't ever come back."

She smiles. "You take care, too." She straddles the snowmobile, snuggles close to the big grizzly man, and rides away.

Steve updates his team, "Wooly's on the way back with Layne Osterman. Repeat, Wooly has Layne Osterman. Entering the trees now."

Fred directs his team from behind a big-ass rock at the half-way point between the road and the cabin, "Mike and Weinstock, get behind Layne's vehicle. Cover your tracks. Move. Move. Move."

The men have taken cover on the far side of Layne's Tahoe when Mike offers a thought, "Hey Fred. The assassin's gonna be armed. Wooly's gonna be a target for Layne if she freaks. You sure you want us back here?"

"Yeah."

"Is Wooly armed?"

"Yeah."

"You think he can handle this?"

"He's ex-CIA."

Mike cracks up, "Only Fred Serpico could find a fucking CIA agent in the wilds of Alaska."

"Rocco sent him."

Mike's new round of laughing is silenced when Wooly drives onto the access road.

The grizzly of a man stops his snowmobile well behind Faulkner's delivery truck.

Layne hops off and scans the road for her Tahoe.

Wooly joins her, "What kind of car are we looking for?"

"Chevy Tahoe. How much snow fell last night?"

"Plenty, but you're probably plowed in. Where do you think you parked?"

Layne scans again and raises her arm toward the spot, "Right—"

Wooly trains his gun on her, "Don't move a fucking muscle, Layne Osterman. Hands behind your head and get on your knees."

Layne pauses, then kneels.

"Hey guys, I've got some firewood to deliver, and you've got a fugitive from justice who needs arresting," Wooly calls out.

The men pop up from behind a snow buried Tahoe, "Happy to help a former CIA agent," Mike smiles wide.

Wooly laughs and makes his way to the provisions truck. He grabs two bundles of wood, slips a piece free, and carries the piles to his ride. He watches Mike place Layne under arrest.

"Flat on the ground, spread your arms and legs," he directs. He places a knee to her back, cuffs her, frisks her, removes two handguns, and Mirandizes her.

Weinstock keeps his gun trained on the assassin until Mike gets her into the delivery truck. The arresting operative seats her in the back adds another set of cuffs, secures them to the back door handle, then gets in the front passenger seat. Weinstock gets on his snowmobile and waits for a call to action.

Wooly gets back on his snowmobile and moves in alone.

# RESCUING LEAVY

Hell hath no fury like a woman scorned—
Earth has Hannah Leavy.

The roar of the approaching snowmobile unleashes a thought, a hope, a belief—*a rescue is underway*. "Replacement delivery man. Forgotten supplies. Return trip. A flash from high in the trees. I need to be ready." She calls to Eli, "I need to use the bathroom."

He moves purposefully into the comfort room, "Can it wait?"

She shakes her head, "No, I'm sorry. Please."

He runs up the stairs, unlocks her, and moves her to the bathroom.

She stays just long enough that he can't return her to the loft.

He moves her to the couch, tosses the keys to her, watches as she locks herself in. "Don't move a fucking muscle Leavy. If you do anything to call attention to yourself, I'll take out the grizzly bear."

"I understand."

Steve updates his team, "I think Leavy knows a rescue is underway. She got Eli to bring her down from the loft. She's sitting on a couch in the fireplace room. She's chained, so someone's gonna have to go in to get her. Wooly doesn't know any of this, but if he gets inside, she'll be more accessible now that she's downstairs. Remember my sniper range, gentlemen."

Wooly pulls to a stop, hops off, and is grabbing one of two bundles of wood from the back.

"I only ordered one," Eli sneers.

"The extra is for the inconvenience."

Eli takes the bundle from Wooly, "I'll be back for the second one."

The ex-CIA agent grabs the piece of wood he set aside and waits. When Eli comes back for the second bundle, Wooly smacks the fuck out of the bastard. "Fuck you, Reynolds." The towering grizzly kicks Eli to make sure the mutha is out cold before entering the cabin.

Steve yells, "Reynolds is down! Move in!"

The roar of snowmobiles coming to life fills the forest.

Wooly makes his way to Leavy who is standing near a wall, "Hannah Leavy, my name is Wooly Jones. I'm ex-CIA working with the RFI team that is barreling toward us. Cover your ears. I'm going to shoot off your chain." Wooly shoots, then grabs Leavy's hand and leads her out the front door. He is immediately whacked across the head with a piece of wood. He falls with the force of a felled tree.

Eli makes a move toward Leavy. She locks her two hands together, circles around, and cuffs him across the face.

He stumbles back and trips over the prone grizzly at his feet.

Leavy dives next to Wooly, searching the snow for the gun that fell free when he hit the ground.

Eli gets onto all fours and moves toward her.

Snowmobiles barrel down on them. There is no shot for the advancing men to take and no shot for the sniper in the trees. They watch Leavy dig through snow as Eli rages toward her from behind. He's pawing for the gun in his pocket— the gun that is no longer in his pocket. He reaches out and grabs Leavy by the chain on her ankle and drags her back. Her hand finds a gun. She rolls onto her back and points it at Eli. "Let go of the fucking chain!"

He lets go and falls onto his ass.

She bolts to her feet and trains the gun on the man she hates most in this world. "Get the fuck up!"

He stays put.

"Get. The. Fuck. Up."

The men dismount their snowmobiles, Steve unperches, and all start running toward Leavy. She points her weapon at them, then immediately back at Eli, "Don't fucking move toward me. You **will not** rescue me!" She turns back to her captor. "Get up, Eli," she says, her voice absent all emotion.

He stands up.

Leavy stares him down. She lowers the gun from chest-height and shoots him between the legs.

He falls to the ground.

"That is for the first time." She moves toward him, stands over him, and shoots him. "That is for Christmas." She knows he's dead, but she shoots him seven more times calling out each of the times he raped her.

Wooly wakes in time for the rage shooting, but doesn't dare move a muscle—even though he is desperate to cover his balls. Fred, Steve, and Weinstock watch the event in silence.

Minutes pass before Weinstock begins his work, "Agent Leavy."

Nothing.

"Leavy."

Nothing.

"Hannah."

Nothing.

He nods to Fred who points his gun at Leavy. Weinstock takes a tentative step toward the woman who's hopelessly gripped by shock. "Agent Leavy, my name is Special Agent Gregory Weinstock. I'd like you to drop your weapon ....... Agent Leavy, your ranking officer demands that you drop your weapon."

Leavy turns her head toward the man's voice and drops the gun. The doctor catches her as she collapses to the ground. He talks softly to the heaving, heaped woman. "Agent, I'm going to help you up and get you inside."

She pitches a fit, "No, no, no! Please, no!"

"Leavy, I'm an FBI agent, and I am also a medical doctor. We need to get you inside. You're barefoot, and there is an ice cold chain wrapped around your ankle which is bleeding pretty badly. We need to warm you up, get the chain removed, and administer care. Do you understand, Leavy?"

She collapses against him.

Weinstock helps her up, walks her into the cabin, and puts her onto the couch. Fred, Steve, and Wooly, search for a key to the lock on her ankle.

Leavy stares blankly—until Fred comes with the key. She tilts her head at the man kneeling before her, "Are you really here?"

The detective tears as he works the lock and removes the chain. "Yes, Leavy, I'm here."

She reaches out and touches his face. "Is Manuel dead?"

"No, Leavy, he's hurt, but he's safe. Just like you, Leavy. You're safe."

"Safe."

*Best numbers ever!*

## One

The head of RFI, the man who has carried the burden of a missing operative, answers a call from Fred Serpico. "Si," he says on bated breath.

"We have Leavy. Eli Reynolds is dead."

Rocco lets out a very long breath that hitches a painful choke of emotion at the end. "Tell me of her condition."

"She's alive, that's really all I can tell you at this time. Weinstock is with her. He sure was needed on this mission."

"When will you be bringing her home?"

"Weinstock wants her to stay put for a couple days. That's based on his assessment of her physical and emotional state. He said she received a recent concussion, has stitches on the back of her head, and she shows signs of addiction, maybe active withdrawal. He wants time to watch her before making a cross country trek."

"Leavy and Weinstock can stay, but I need you, Mike, and Steve back ASAP. The feces is flinging and finding whirling devices."

Fred laughs big—and it feels good. "If the shit is hitting the fan, you'd better take cover."

"Si, I am below my desk as we speak."

"You need to come out from under, Rocco, and start thinking about how you want to handle the capture of Layne Osterman, 'cause we got her, too."

Bang. "Shit!"

"Bumped your head, did you?"

"No, my hand upon my desk. Goddamn good work, Fred Chester Serpico."

Fred's growl could be heard from Alaska sans the cell phone. "I was going to bring her to The Compound, but I might give her to the FBI."

"Point received. There will be no more mention of your middle name, Detective Serpico. You handle the transport of the prisoner to The Compound. Leave Dr. Weinstock and Wooly Jones with Leavy. The doctor can let us know when she's ready for return. Leavy's recue and Layne's capture are your stories to tell, Fred, so have at it."

"Thanks, Rocco."

### Two

"Randall."

"Fred."

"We have Leavy." Fred listens to The Kid break over the phone and then to dead air.

### Three

"Malcolm."

"Fred."

"We have Leavy."

"Thank God. Will her road back be a long one?"

"If she makes it back, Malcolm, it will be a very long one." Fred listens to Malcolm center himself, then to prolonged silence.

Malcolm breaks the silence, "Fred, there's something else on your mind."

"We captured Layne Osterman."

Silence. Anguish. **The** question. "Where is she?"

"We're taking her to The Compound. No one knows we have her—no one but the RFI family even knows who she is."

"I want her brought to justice, Fred."

"Understood. Rocco is gonna want to get whatever he can before he turns her over to the FBI. I'm sorry to add to your load, Malcolm, but you can't say anything to anyone."

"Understood."

"Again, I'm sorry to add to your load, but you might want to check in with The Kid. He's wrapped pretty tight over Leavy."

"On it. Thank you, Fred."

Four

"John."

"Fred."

"We have Leavy."

Barely held emotion pushes John's next question. "Condition, Fred?"

"Fucked up."

Fred waits while John breaks a bit.

Leavy's former lover offers the only thing he has—hope, "She's strong, Fred."

"Not sure anyone's strong enough for what she went through."

"Fuck, Fred."

"She's gonna need us—all of us, John. Some good news from this cesspool mission— we have Osterman."

"I didn't hear that," he says before hanging up.

## 275

Malcolm knocks on Randy's apartment door, "Fred said I should check on you, so open up."

The Kid opens the door as a big smile crosses his face, "Yo, didn't know the Detecting One cared, and I don't know what that emotional tsunami was about. It's not like Leavy fucked up her knee, ended her NBA career, and broke my heart."

Malcolm roars in laughter until his own tears start.

A very confused Gretchen finds the two men of the manor vacillating between laughter and tears, "What on God's green earth is taking place?"

"They found Leavy," the men say in unison.

Gretchen runs to the men's arms and laughs until she cries, then she cries until she laughs.

*Beware Rocco-speak.*


Manuel Xavier takes one look at his father and runs from the track, "Leavy," he pants.

"Si. We have her."

Manuel breaks, bends as though he's been sucker-punched.

"We'll sit and talk." The men make their way to a bench. "Fred and his team found her in a cabin in an area of Kenai National Wildlife Refuge."

"A needle in a haystack."

"Si."

Silence.

The son readies himself to ask the question.

The father readies himself to answer it.

"She's been hurt?"

"Si."

"Badly?"

"Si."

Manuel cannot bring himself to ask anything else.

Rocco slaps his boy's shoulder, "I've called a meeting to tell the others. Come if you want."

The silence is deafening when Rocco enters the great room. He smiles wide. "Leavy will be coming home."

The building erupts in celebration. Tears, hugs, tears, laughter, tears, sadness, tears, reality. A whirlwind of collective relief and joy turns to moments of individual reflection and concern.

Rocco steps in when the RFI family realizes bringing Leavy home is only the first step toward reunification. "I spoke with Fred. He said that Leavy is under the physical and emotional care of Dr. Weinstock. The doctor has suggested she stay put for a day or two before coming back. Plans will be made for Leavy based on **her** needs. There will be no other considerations."

All eyes turn toward Manuel who has found his way to the top of the stairs. He slumps back against a wall and hangs his head.

Rocco presses on. "There is other important news. The RFI jet will be returning sometime within the next 12 hours. It will be bringing Fred, Steve, and Mike home. Accompanying them is the assassin of Senator Curtis Morgan."

The room stills, breaths are held, and thoughts run deep.

Rocco sets the rules. "Until further notice, this Compound is armed 24/7 and is on a full communications lockdown, except at the

Computer Center. The only phone calls or texts sanctioned from inside the fortress are to RFI members, or to John Maxwell or Shelby Webber. When Layne Osterman is delivered, we will have two criminal elements within our Compound. Neither woman will be informed of the other's presence. The women will be kept separate from one another. The women will be given no information from outside these premises. Guards will be assigned to these criminals 24/7. Team members with legitimate bitchiness with Felicity Ferraro or Layne Osterman are not allowed proximity.

"As for the assassin, she will be confined to the Computer Center. Admittance is allowed for the following people only: Gia, Fred, Steve, Mike, Annie, and me. If our guest leaves her quarters, shoot to injure if you can. Penny, Ted, and Master Michael will be going out on an assignment in the next 24 to 36." Rocco paces back and forth in front of the fireplace, then stops and extends his hand to his wife. All eyes and ears are on the married couple. "When Leavy returns, she will be staying in the medical suite. Manuel will be staying with her if that is what she wants. Dr. Weinstock will be her primary resource. Maura, I'd like you to work with Weinstock, unless Leavy objects. Our loved one has been under the control of a nefarious one. She needs to take back control. She will do that by making decisions for herself. We will follow her lead. No one is allowed in the medical suite unless they are requested to be there. If Leavy bonds with someone and she needs them with her, we will take over that person's responsibilities. Having said that, Maura and Steve will need help with the twins."

"On it, Rocco."

"Grazie, Kitt."

"We have a long road with Leavy. Caring for her and helping her along is for another day. Tonight, I want you all to rejoice that she is back in loving arms."

Rocco and Joy leave,
and speak only when they get outside.

"The shit is hitting the fan, Rocco."

"Si, that is what I told Fred."

"I can only imagine the Rocco-speak on that American saying."

He laughs until they enter the Computer Center and Joy turns on the overhead screen and flips through the channels…

**"… FBI sources reveal a cell phone was found at the suicide scene of Carter Thorndyke, former secretary of Homeland Security. It is confirmed that the phone belonged to the deceased man. According to the same FBI source several prominent government officials placed calls to Thorndyke the**

morning of his suicide. Names of those officials have not yet been released ......."

"... Roland Gaffney, former Director of FICA and one of the leaders of the criminal organization known as The Realm, was found dead in his solitary confinement cell in an undisclosed Federal prison ......."

"... Antonio Alvarez, Peruvian crime lord and one of the leaders of the criminal organization known as The Realm, was found dead in his solitary confinement cell at the ADX super-max penitentiary in Florence, Colorado ......."

"As I told Fred, the feces is flinging and finding whirling devices."

"Oh God, it's worse than I thought."

*Slinging the slang.*

Turner Rodgers is behind closed doors watching, listening, and bending his elbow, plenty. Within minutes of another round of breaking news reports, his cell phone rings. He knows it's The Body.

"What a pleasant surprise, Mathis."

"Where is Felicity?"

"Still don't know. If Thorndyke took her, you may never find her. He's dead, you know." Turner's laugh is a bit on the unhinged side of things.

"Your panic is showing, Turner. Perhaps you are one of the prominent government officials who called Thorndyke the morning of his death."

"Fuck you, Mathis."

"Roland Gaffney is dead."

"Fuck you, Mathis."

"Antonio Alvarez is dead."

"Fuck you, Mathis."

"You are dead if you or any of the remaining Gang members mention Felicity Ferraro to the authorities. If she is still alive, I want her to walk away from this."

There is silence on the line.

"Are you still there, Turner?"

"The Gang isn't going to go down for this without taking her with them," Turner snarls.

"Listen the fuck up, Turner. The first indication that someone has flipped on Felicity, I will release all of the information I have on all of you and not just The Realm stuff. Sterility issues, the diddling with minors, the inside tracks of drug abuse—it **all** comes to light. Do you understand?"

"Yes."

"Make sure the others understand. Not one word, Turner."

The Compound

Rocco visits The Widow at the medical suite. "We have work to do and plans for you are underway."

"Does the work have anything to do with your search for my children or the threat Mathis left in my safe?"

"Both."

"What are your plans?"

"We are sending you back to DC, Mrs. Ferraro."

"I can't go back."

"Get dressed. Your guard will escort you to my office for explanations."

Rocco and Joy are ending an embrace when Felicity strolls in.

"Huh. You're not at all what I expected, Mrs. Fiancetti. The great and powerful DOA is a bit on the wee side."

Joy doesn't bite. "Sit down. Quite a bit has happened since you've arrived at the Fiancetti Compound. Shortly after the FBI announced your kidnapping, Carter Thorndyke blew his brains out."

The Widow smiles.

"If that amuses you, Mrs. Ferraro, you'll love the next part. Shortly before Thorndyke ended it all, he received telephone calls from the following people: Thomas Haley, Eugene Jackson, Christie Sargent, Stephanie Butler, Robert Cantor, and Turner Rodgers."

The Widow laughs.

"And Mathis Reynolds."

The Widow stops laughing.

"This is what happened overnight. Roland Gaffney and Antonio Alvarez were found dead in their solitary confinement cells in two different Federal prisons in two different states."

The Widow squirms.

"Someone is very busy snipping loose ends. Word around DC is that Mathis Reynolds is looking for you. He's been putting pressure on Turner Rodgers to find out who took you. In the immediate ensuing hours of your kidnapping, the most likely candidate was Thorndyke, but his suicide called into question his culpability. Still, he may have ordered your abduction and your murder then decided to end it all, but without your dead body, Mathis Reynolds is left to wonder what really happened. It's only a matter of time before he wonders whether you're in protective custody spilling your guts. Our dilemma is that we either produce your dead body, or we send you back. Your choice."

The Widow laughs—a bit too loudly and way too insanely. "You're a bit of a chancer, aren't you Joy Ann **Watts**. Allowing the enemy within your fortress. You think I'm a thick one? Catch yourself on, you should. I've a plan, and you two sauntered in."

"What's with the Irish slang?"

"You'd prefer the native Gaelic? Airson rudan nach 'm f chumail."

"For things aren't what they seem," Joy translates.

"For any of us, Mrs. Fiancetti."

*Is that what we're calling it now?*

Gretchen has been in her office inside campaign headquarters all day. Baby Girl is swaying to and fro in a musical swing having just finished her feeding. Momma and daughter are surrounded by whiteboards covered with sectioned maps colored in varying shades of red, blue, and purple—charts and graphs tracking polling numbers, election day filing deadlines and requirements for states across the U.S., and a checklist of other things on Gretchen's plate. She picks up her vibrating cell, quickly checks to see if it disturbed her sleeping baby, and answers it with a happy, "Hello, Madam co-chair."

Madison Morgan brightens at the title, "Hello, Gretchen. I read your email and am very impressed at how many ducks you have in a row. Tell me how I can best serve you."

"Let me tell you what falls outside my comfort zone, and you tell me if it's something you are interested in handling."

"Very well."

"The Federal Contributions Limits. I know we touched on it when we filed the Statement of Candidacy, but I could easily see a distraction on this end interfering with my due diligence. It's way too important so I'm hoping you could track the money. I have a handle on the state filing requirements and deadlines and Peyton Wells is going to help coordinate that effort, but I could always send her to you in Georgia. And you are always welcome here if that's something you'd like. In any event, Peyton can help with the contributions if need be."

"Very well. Why don't I focus on the contributions limits and have Peyton visit here when the volume picks up. I can do a tutorial, and she can be my backup. And I have Bertha who is ready, willing, and able."

"An absolutely wonderful idea having Bertha help out. Madison, there's something else. I don't need your help per se, but your insight is most welcome. I've a thought about Malcolm participating in both the Democratic and Republican debates. I've been looking at the 2020 projected map, and I see several areas where he could make inroads in both camps, and maybe we use the debates to create awareness."

"Go on."

"Pennsylvania for starters; it's Malcolm's home state, but in the last presidential election 9.2 percent of Obama voters became Trump Democrats. By and large the Democrats who voted Republican in 2016 said they saw Trump as the change candidate. They may be interested in changing back in 2020."

Madison pauses, then opines. "There will be some voters who think Malcolm is as politically inexperienced as Trump was, but when the electorate hears Malcolm speak, they will recognize the differences in the two men. Malcolm's intelligence and impassioned vision for the country will shine through. I think you are right to expect a significant return of those Pennsylvania voters."

"There are other states I want to discuss further, but I want to mention Texas now. The latest Gallup poll has Texas registered voters standing at 20 percent liberal and 35 percent moderate. I think this bodes well for Malcolm, as 77 still carries positive weight in the Lone Star State. Of course, there will be some who will rightly sully him because of the way he handled the Sage Finley matter when she was first killed. I think public sentiment will swing his way, though. We'll keep reminding them that when he got his head on straight, he did the right thing. Let's not forget that he moved heaven and earth to find Micky Strong and bring him to justice. I think most Texans and Americans will come to his place on that matter."

Madison's voice sings with pride. "Gretchen, I think you have politics in your blood. Given Malcolm's strong poll numbers, and his draw from both sides of the political aisle, I think you are right to consider debating with both sides. The Commission on Presidential

Debates, isn't inclined to agree, however. Further, the DNC and RNC will not want Malcolm on their stage."

Gretchen is nodding while Madison speaks. "Right, but a 2000 CPD rule says a third-party candidate can be included in the national debates if he or she garners at least 15 percent support across five national polls. By the time the general election debates roll around, he'll be there. Besides, there's been a lot of controversy and public support in previous elections to let third-party candidates in. I think Malcolm is the poster-boy candidate for this issue. If we move on this, there is a local reporter who will carry his water effectively."

"Gretchen, let me put some thought into this and ask a few people in the know on this issue. I'll talk to you tomorrow. By the way, have you told Malcolm about our working together?"

"The next time I lay eyes on my man, I'll be telling him."

"Telling him what?" Malcolm says from the doorway.

"Oh, Madison, Malcolm just walked in. I'll call you back." Gretchen gets up and moves toward him, "How long have you been standing there?"

"Since you said, 'Hello, Madam co-chair.'"

"So you know. What do you think?"

"Inspired." Malcolm walks into Gretchen's office, "I have a meeting in a few minutes, but I'd like you to tell me more about the debates and the states where you see inroads. Jim Morrisey, my Democratic opponent, is my biggest challenge since I think Turner Rodgers will be in legal jeopardy by then."

"Any idea who will step in if he bows out?"

"The GOP field is bloodied from the division caused by the current head of the Party, and Turner isn't helping their cause. We should prepare a strategy for a centrist and also a far-right candidate."

Gretchen takes a seat, extends her long legs, runs her fingers through her cropped hair, and pulls a deep breath that has her girls saying, "look at me, look at me." She vixens her man with a long smoldering look and slowly skims her tongue over her top lip, "My very biased opinion, Mr. Price, is that there isn't a man alive who could best you in the face department." Her eyes run the length of him, and settle for a long look on his very long erection, "As for that, there isn't a woman in the world who could resist that."

Malcolm leans back against the wall, "Come here, Woman."

Gretchen sashays toward her man, unbuttoning and untucking her blouse along the way. She flips the lock on her office door. His eyes hood, and a slow, deep growl, or two is heard from his corner. "Don't move," she unzips his pants. She giggles, "Mr. Mayor, I see your polls are up."

"Is that what we're calling it now?"

Gretchen drops her head back in laughter, which is immediately caught on a moan when her husband lifts her skirt and pushes her panties aside.

# Snowfall Prison

Wooldruff Jones returns to Cabin 5, having handled the disposal of Eli Reynolds. He is fresh out of a shower, wafting a 'clean as a whistle' scent, dressed in fresh attire, and sporting a bandage across his forehead. He shuffles into the room pronouncing, "Took out the trash, now I'm looking for a whiskey." He notices Leavy fast asleep on a mattress in front of the fireplace, and quickly lowers his voice, "Sorry, didn't know the Miss was sleeping."

Dr. Weinstock holds up a bottle of pills, "Not sleeping so much as sedated."

"Did you bring those with you, Doc?"

"Nope. I brought many things that could have aided Leavy, but she said she's been drugged since she got here. It's best to keep her on the same pills for now. She consented to taking a lower dose."

"Do you think she's addicted?" Wooly asks.

"Yes. Operative Leavy will be facing many challenges when we get back to The Compound. Her addiction is at the top of the list."

# Dickless

The RFI team from Alaska arrives in Halifax, climbs into a waiting Land Rover, and makes the trip to The Compound in silence. The accompanying assassin has been prohibited from hearing or seeing anything during flight and during ground transport. As soon as her feet hit Fiancetti turf, she is brought to the small bedroom at the back of the Computer Center through a back entrance. Rocco is waiting inside. "Ah, the assassin has arrived. Please take a seat. We will communicate for a few minutes before I attend business."

Layne is escorted to a table that has a covered serving dish and a plastic drinking glass.

Rocco uncovers the plate, "My team informs me that you have not eaten since your arrest. If you change your mind, feel free to partake. It's quite good."

"It's probably poisoned."

Rocco laughs, "Ms. Osterman, you have been in the company of RFI men who could have killed you many times over. If we wanted you dead, you would be dead."

Layne makes no move toward the food.

Rocco smiles, "Perhaps later, then. You will be held here for 36 hours, then turned over to the FBI for the killings of Benton Brettenvue, EMTs Robert Arsenault and Adam Booker, physical therapist Kelly Thompson, the attempted murder of Penny Meehan, and the execution of Senator Curtis Morgan. What happens to you will be decided by others, but I suspect this may be your fate." Rocco turns on a wall-mounted television.

**"...Roland Gaffney and Antonio Alvarez were murdered while in solitary confinement at maximum security Federal prisons."**

Layne scoffs, "That could have been created for my benefit."

Rocco flips the channel. CNN, FOX, NBC, ABC, CBS—they are all running the same information. "Check the date and time at the bottom of each broadcast, Ms. Osterman. You will see it corresponds with the time on the wall clock. Let's watch the minutes pass together."

"What do you want?"

Rocco smiles. "Information which RFI has not already uncovered. If you are able to provide, I will request that you be kept in solitary confinement. It may not help you long-term, given The Realm's proclivity for assassinations, but—"

The captive laughs at the jab. "I want something else."

"Proceed."

"I want to see my Daddy within 48-hours of my being turned over to the FBI. I want a thirty minute visit."

Rocco nods.

"I am not sure what you already know, but I'll talk."

Rocco heads toward the exit, "Eat and sleep first. I will return in the morning. If you make any move to escape we will become your assassins. Goodnight, Ms. Osterman." He stops at the door, "Steve, you and two others are on guard duty. The entrance between the bedroom and Center is locked from the other side. Guard from inside this room. If the prisoner blinks funny, shoot her."

Rocco meets Fred, Ted and Mike outside, "Ted you're on this door. If Layne Osterman steps through it, and she is not accompanied by Steve, shoot her. Master Michael, you are going out on an assignment in the morning with Ted and Penny. You will be returning the trash to the States. There is an information packet at your cottage. You are heading this mission, Michael. Please devise a plan and inform me tomorrow. Annie is working at the Main Cottage tonight."

"Until what time?"

"Seven antemeridian."

"Tell Sweet Annie I'll expect her in my bed at five past seven antemeridian," his growl cutting the thick forest as he makes his way through.

"I'm not telling her," Fred calls out.

Rocco laughs, "I'll have Gia tell her."

The men head to the office near the medical suite. Annie is guarding The Widow's room, Penny is riding a wall. Fred opens his arms to his friend and she walks right in.

"Is she here?"

"Yes. You need to stay away from her, Penny."

"I will."

Her new boss jumps into the conversation, "Centesimo, you and Ted will be going on an assignment with Mike tomorrow. Your man is on Osterman guard duty tonight, then he will get shuteye, then the three of you will be moving out. Now, please ask Manuel to join us in my office."

Fred kisses the top of Penny's head before releasing her from his embrace, "Be safe."

"I'm telling my mother you've got a thing for Penny," Annie calls after him.

"She already knows, Pixie."

Manuel sprints into the office, "Fred. You saw her?"

"I did."

"You saw her," Manuel breaks a bit.

Fred breaks a bit.

"Son, sit while Fred tells us of Alaska. Things will not settle well, Manuel, so manage yourself."

Fred exhales big then begins. "The team identified two long-stay cabins inside Kenai National Wildlife Refuge where women were staying. We worked a way to get near, then an hour or so before we were to move in, we learned that Layne Osterman was in the area of Cabin 5. That put us on notice about where we'd find Leavy. We perched Steve so he could scope the cabin and report back. He got an immediate view of Leavy sitting near a window in a second-story loft. He reported that she might have seen a flash from his gear and may even have known there was a rescue plan underway. She got Eli to move her to the first floor and did her part even though she was chained at the ankle."

Manuel drops his head, but remains silent.

"Earlier in the week, I happened upon Wooly Jones, a man posing as wildlife refuge manager, He's actually ex-CIA."

Manuel laughs and addresses his father, "A friend of yours."

"Si."

"Wooly arranged with a dude named Fletch Faulkner—"

"Sorry for the interruption, Fred, but Fletch is the real refuge manager and also Wooly's son-in-law."

"Good to know. Now, no more interruptions. The plan was for Wooly to go to the cabin to do a provisions delivery, and if the feces hit whirling devices while he was there, he had orders to take out Layne and Steve would take out Eli. When Eli learned Wooly forgot to bring firewood to the cabin and had to go back to the provision's truck, he asked if Layne could hitch a ride to her truck parked on the access road, Wooly pulled his weapon on Layne—"

"Ah, Bessie."

"...and ordered her to the ground. Mike made the arrest, cuffed her, and locked her inside the provisions truck. While Mike was doing his thing with Osterman, Wooly was loading two bundles of firewood onto his snowmobile. He slipped one of the pieces out and put it up front with him. I followed him to the tree line and watched along with Steve, who communicated every move everyone made. When Wooly got to the cabin he hopped off and handed Eli a bundle of wood, and told him he brought an extra one because of the inconvenience. Eli brought the first bundle inside and when he came back for the second one, Wooly knocked the fucker out cold. Wooly went into the cabin, identified himself to Leavy, shot the chain from her ankle and ran her out. By then, Eli had come around and before Steve could get a clear shot, he grabbed the wood, knocked Wooly out, and made a grab for Leavy who locked her hands, spun around and fucked up his nose but good. While his ass was on the ground, she started  searching the snow for Wooly's gun. Eli crawled toward her, grabbed onto the length of chain on her ankle and started pulling her toward him. Somehow she found the gun, rolled onto her back, pointed it at Eli and ordered him away. She got to her feet and trained the gun on the downed man. By this time, we were off our snowmobiles and ready to help her. She turned the weapon on us for a fraction of a second and demanded that none of us rescue her." Fred stops and looks at Rocco, who nods and warns his son again.

"Manage yourself."

Manuel remains silent—he fumes, but he does it silently.

Fred stares off, gives his head a good shake, "Leavy told Eli to get the fuck up! Twice. After a bit, he stood up. She stared him down, lowered the gun from a chest aim and shot his dick off. He fell to the ground. She told him that that was for the first time. She moved toward him, stood over him, and shot him again and said that was for Christmas. He was dead by then, but she shot him seven more times calling out every time he raped her."

Fred lets silence swallow the emotions of his listeners.

# FRED AND KITT

Fred's heart bangs hard when he sees his woman sitting on the top stair just outside the great room. "Kittridge." He approaches slowly, still somewhat unsure of things. "Are you lost?"

She smiles, "No."

"Tired?"

"No."

"Are you waiting on me?"

"Always."

"Sure glad to hear it." He makes his way halfway up the stairs and parks his ass on one. "Cramped quarters, Kittridge."

"Not for me, Fred."

He laughs, "I suppose there's a reason we're hanging here."

"Joseph, Charlotte, Noah, and Cordelia are having a sleep-together in the great room, and I'm on guard duty."

"Dangerous mission. Where's your backup?"

"He just arrived," she laughs.

His heart bangs again. "I've missed you, Kittridge. I've missed us."

She gives him one of her million-watt smiles, "While you've been off looking for Leavy, I've been here looking for myself. I want to tell you what happened and why I responded the way I did, why I pushed you away." She tears a bit, wipes one or two that find their way south. "I started having a problem with flashbacks last spring. They began right after you returned from Penobscot Bay with a gunshot wound. Over time, they subsided, or I learned how to manage them. They started again after Stacy Remington was killed, and then became a constant after Manuel was shot and Leavy was taken." She pulls a few unsteady breaths before continuing. "The manageable flashbacks turned into barely manageable panic attacks that were triggered by sounds from the firing range. Every shot seemed to unleash a reaction: flinching, sweating, shaking, and the interval between shots determined how bad the attack was. After a while, I was gripped by a never-ending uneasiness. The only respite I had was when I'd take Joseph on our woodland walks because when we were on the trails, the firing range was shut down. The Compound was peaceful and quiet. My rambles with our son became longer and more frequent, and they were really helping—until the day of the breach onto RFI property."

Fred makes a move to comfort her when she breaks.

Kitt stops him, "Don't. Please." She rides the emotional wave, then settles herself. "I want you to know that I was terrified when those men were nearing me in the woods, but I also want you to know that I took care of our son." She waits for his acknowledgement.

"I know, Kittridge."

"When Joey and I were back safe and sound, something inside me broke. I got really pissed. The way I replayed the events in my head was that I cowered in the bitter cold rather than taking action, that I had to be rescued by the RFI team, rather than rescuing myself." She bats a few tears away, "I got **really** pissed when you flew back to tend to the little woman." She stares at Fred, "Aren't you going to ask me why that pissed me off?"

"I wasn't sure this was a give and take, Kittridge, but since you brought it up, I'd like to know." He already knows.

"I blamed you for the way I was feeling. You getting shot left me feeling vulnerable, insecure, and out of control. I didn't like the feelings. I didn't know how to work through them, and I couldn't ask for help."

"Why?" He already knows.

"Because I'm surrounded by people who aren't vulnerable, who know nothing about feeling insecure, and who are in control every minute of every day. I believed there wasn't anyone who would understand—no one who could, or should, be asked to handle this issue—especially when there are so many more pressing issues, like finding a missing RFI family member." She breaks.

He breaks for her. He waits for her.

"See," she sobs. "Leavy was kidnapped by evil, evil people. And Kitt is feeling—" She breaks.

He breaks with her. He waits for her.

"I'm not sure whether Steve told you, but he and I had words, and by that I mean he tried to help, and I left my rage at his feet."

"First I'm hearing about this."

"Not surprising since I shamed him for telling you about the scare in the woods."

"Kittridge, I'm second in command at this facility. I had to be told about the breach."

"That's what Steve said, and I knew that deep down, but it felt like a betrayal. It felt like one more thing was out of my control. I was out of control, Fred, or moving steadfastly in that direction. When Steve pushed me to talk to him, I said some things I didn't even know I felt."

"Like?"

"That I don't belong here. That I have no purpose here. I'm not a champion for the greater good; I'm a spectator, a cheerleader, a ward of the state of RFI. I haven't any freedoms and no say in anything. Every minute of my every day needs to fit in and around everyone else at this fortress, even my daily trek has to be scheduled and sanctioned. The scare in the woods threatened that little bit of enjoyment. I really felt there was nothing left, no reason for me to stay here. I pushed you and everyone else away because I needed to find a reason to stay or a way to leave." She abandons the top stair and moves to the one just above Fred. "When you asked me to leave the life I'd built at Bullet Bungalow and begin a life here with you and everyone else I hold near and dear, I did that for you. I pretended otherwise, but I did that for you. Pushing you away, so I could make my own decision about living and thriving here, I did for myself." She crawls onto Fred's lap and traces every contour of his face. "I know how deeply you love me, and that you would leave RFI if I asked. I also know you hoped that I would find my way to staying here. You should know that what you wanted was not part of my decision-making process. I didn't give you one single thought."

His smile is so wide, it looks painful. "Not sure why that makes me happy, but—"

She traces his long-line dimples, "I love you, Fred Serpico. I love being your woman, a mother, a writer, a friend, and a member of this community. When I got really deep in the weeds thinking about my life, I realized that the only person questioning whether I belonged here was me. Everyone accepts me for who I am, they appreciate my contributions, and they see me as something other than someone you brought along for the ride. And you should know that I've found that I quite enjoy shooting shit and dabbling in hand to hand combat. Want to hit the mats, big boy."

"Good God, Woman, I'll take you on these damned stairs if that's what you want." Fred Serpico laughs big!

"Airson rudan nach 'm f chumail."


Rocco, Mike, Ted, and Penny are quietly caffeinating themselves at the kitchen table when Fred saunters in on a yawn, "Coffee." He pours. He sits. He listens.

"Master Michael, what is your plan for The Widow?"

"The RFI jet will fly us to a tiny airstrip in Cullen, Virginia. We'll drive The Widow to Culpeper, which is 72 miles from DC. I researched Carter Thorndyke last night and found an article that mentions his fondness of Culpeper. In the article the UVA graduate said he fell in love with Virginia the moment he saw Culpeper. I think it's enough to connect Thorndyke to the abduction by putting The Widow in that neck of the woods."

"Si. And The Widow, what are your plans?"

"Joy and Maura are dirtying her up a bit, so her appearance suggests some time in unpleasant surroundings. She will be cuffed on the jet, and after she memorizes this script, she'll be given a mild sedative. When we land in Virginia, we'll drop her off along some quiet road."

Rocco reads the script out loud, "Kidnapped. Taken to the Peppers. Let me go."

"It will be her mantra. We want the locals to find her, recognize her confusion, and take her to a hospital. A blood test will show sedatives in her system. The locals will start researching her and asking questions. Everything from that point is up to Mrs. Ferraro."

Maura raises a skeptical brow, "Are you sure about this, Mrs. Ferraro?"

"Just do it. It'll make the whole kidnapping thing more believable."

Maura seeks approval from Joy.

"Her call." Joy hands Maura a pair of scissors and continues video recording the events.

Maura bands The Widow's hair and quickly cuts off the gathered ponytail. The cut is jagged and uneven.

The Widow smiles and proclaims, "I love it."

"Oh, for fuck's sake," Joy responds.

"Now for the black eye," The Widow says.

"Can I do that?" Maura asks.

"Be my guest."

"No, Mrs. Fiancetti. You will do it."

"Not a good call, Mrs. Ferraro. It'll be a lot worse coming from me."

"As will my return strike—not given today, of course, but one day." Felicity Ferraro is barely standing from her chair when Joy delivers the blow. "No warning. Fair play will be a bitch, Mrs. Fiancetti."

Joy laughs as she tosses a pair of dirty sweat pants, T-shirt, and smelly sneakers at The Widow.

She looks at the lot, "Are these yours?"

Joy laughs, "Hardly."

She repeats the question to Maura.

"No, but I helped pull them from the town dump. They don't belong to anyone at The Compound. When they are checked for DNA it's anyone's guess whose will register."

"You're leaving in ten minutes, so get dressed. And I hope never to see you again, Mrs. Ferraro."

Felicity laughs, "Hope springs eternal, Mrs. Fiancetti. Remember these words, "Airson rudan nach 'm f chumail."

"Maura, please tell Mike the trash is ready for dumping."

# Snowfall Prison

Leavy wakes, though she is unable to grab hold of her faculties. Snippets of thoughts flash behind her tightly closed eyes. She opens one at a time, gently blinks away scratchiness while she struggles to orient. "Mattress. On the floor." Panic seizes. "Warehouse? Dan Shea?" Clarity inches its way through her fuzzy brain. "No, I'm in the cabin with my other kidnapper," she tears. She stills herself, "Don't let him know you're awake—but I have to pee," she whimpers. Leavy rolls onto her back, moves her legs back and forth expecting the pull upon one of them. "No chain?" She rolls onto her side again and pushes up, turns to search for Eli, but finds a strange man asleep on the couch instead. She screams and scrambles into a corner and crouches by the fireplace.

The man on the couch bolts upright. A second man charges from a back bedroom. Both men train their guns for a single second. Weinstock hands his off to Wooly then begins a tentative approach, "Good morning, Leavy. I'm Dr. Weinstock. We met the other day."

The terrified woman's eyes dart wildly as memories attack. She lowers herself from a crouched position to a sitting one, still pressed tight into a corner. She feels something wet beneath her and starts to cry when she realizes she's peed herself. "I need help," she whispers.

The doctor moves to her, "May I sit?"

She nods.

"Tell me what you need, Leavy."

After many minutes, she leans in and whispers, "I need to ask about Manuel." She begins shaking her head, her voice changes tone and tempo, **"What are the rules, Leavy?"** Her voice cracks, "Don't try to escape. Don't try to engage with others. Don't ask about Manuel." She breaks, and when she rights herself she asks, "Am I still at Snowfall Prison?"

"You are still in the cabin, but you are free now. There is no one here who will hurt you." Weinstock puts his hand palm up on his thigh, "Leavy would you like to hold my hand?"

She slips hers into his and wraps her fingers tight. "Eli? Is he gone?"

"Yes."

"Will he come back?"

"No."

"Did I kill him?"

"Yes."

"Good. If I didn't kill him, it would have been ten."

Weinstock remains silent. He lets her work the reasons for her actions through on her own.

"He was going to rape me after Layne left. He told me. He was going to rape me." She turns wetting eyes to the stranger who's sitting in a puddle of her piss holding her hand. "He didn't get the chance."

"No, Leavy, he didn't." She puts her head onto Weinstocks shoulder and cries herself to sleep.

Wooly grabs his coat and heads outside to answer his phone, "What?"

Fred laughs, "What the fuck crawled up your butt?"

"Eli Reynolds and what he did to that poor Miss."

Fred swallows the lump that fills his throat, "I'm glad she blew off his balls."

"She doesn't remember it. She's cowering in the corner in piss soaked pants, saying he had plans to rape her as soon as Layne left. One good thing though, she let Weinstock sit with her. She cried herself to sleep on his shoulder."

"Well, fuck, Wooly, I'm sure glad I called you first thing."

Wooly laughs, "What do you want Fred?"

"Your friend, Rocco Fiancetti, wants to know if you can stay with Weinstock and Leavy until they are ready to fly home?"

"Planned on it."

"He also wants to know if you'll come back with them?"

"Planned on it."

"Yeah, figured as much. See you soon."

"Plan on it, Detecting One."

*Piccolo, si?*

A patrol car pulls behind a stumbling woman two miles from the center of Culpeper, Virginia. The officer behind the wheel puts his lights on hoping to get her attention without scaring her. The Widow turns, stumbles, tries to right herself, and falls to the ground. The officer runs to her aid. "Ma'am. Are you injured? Let me help you up." The officer leans in to hear what she is saying.

"Kidnapped. Taken to the Peppers. Let me go. Kidnapped. Taken to the Peppers. Let me go."

"Ma'am, I'm going to get you to the hospital. Please have a seat in the back of my cruiser."

Felicity Ferraro says little during the ER exam, and when she tries to feed herself some beef broth, she notices the tremble of her hand. When the medical personnel leave her alone in a private, police guarded hospital room she loses it a bit. Full-on body shakes precede a full-on panic attack when she sees her image cross the television screen with the breaking news banner, **Kidnapped DC Woman Found in Virginia.** "I need to get out of here and back home before someone finds me and kills me."

Alexandria

John Maxwell and Shelby Webber are on a conference call with Rocco Fiancetti when the news about Felicity Ferraro breaks. John hands Shelby a glass of wine and clinks his beer bottle against it, then has second thoughts. "Rocco, are we supposed to be okay with The Widow walking away scot-free?"

"Ah, a good question. The FBI has considerable things to investigate and criminals to prosecute, si?"

"Si," Shelby answers. "As soon as the dam breaks we should be able to arrest the remaining members of the Gang. So far, these esteemed criminals are banding together. I've waved an offer of full immunity to the first one who flips. I let them know I **really** want Turner Rodgers, but no one's talking yet. They're probably hoping for a Presidential pardon and won't come running until Turner's poll numbers bottom out. We've got the goods on them, but we can't use everything we have without putting Felicity Ferraro at the center of the leak. Until her children are found, we will not jeopardize their safety. In the meantime, we will play cat to the DC rats."

"My appreciations, Director. Have any of the rodents mentioned Mrs. Ferraro's involvement?"

"Not one."

"Ah, I suspect Mathis Reynolds has put them on notice. I've read the files Mrs. Ferraro had on the malefactors. If Mathis has those files, he has all the leverage he needs to keep them in line."

The director lowers her voice a bit. "Rocco, when we move on the Gang, we will be using those files. Personally speaking, I can't wait to press Turner Rodgers on the paternity/sterility issue. That seemingly inconsequential matter must be explosive for him to try to hide it all these years and to throw in with the treasonous Realm."

John nudges Shelby, "Your interest seems awfully close to wanting in on the gossip of the decade, ma'am."

"Uh huh, I totally want to know."

Rocco interrupts the banter of friends, "I assure you, Shelby, when the paternity of Turner Rodgers' children is revealed, it will not be inconsequential."

"YOU KNOW?" Shelby and John yell.

Shelby nudges her man, "You seem very interested in this bit of gossip."

Rocco laughs heartedly. "I believe we have other matters to discuss, Director."

"Of course, now that The Realm pieces are fitting together, tell me when we will be getting Layne Osterman."

Rocco pulls a deep breath, "Si, about that..."

"Oh, God," John mutters.

"Ah, the Annoying One knows what is coming."

"You made assurances with her."

"Si, but it is piccolo in nature. In return for her guilty pleas in the death of Senator Curtis Morgan, and the remainder of her atrocities, the assassin wants a 30 minute face to face meeting with her father within 48-hours of her arrest by the FBI. Piccolo, si?"

John and Shelby clink their drinks again, "Piccolo, si."

Shelby continues talking, "Tell me, Rocco, what will you be doing with your time now that Agent Leavy has been rescued, Layne Osterman is behind bars, and The Realm and its leaders are finished?"

"I am going to search the world for Mathis Reynolds and Felicity Ferraro."

"You think they will end up together?" Shelby asks.

"Si. They belong together. Just like you and Caligula. Caio," Rocco says on a roaring laugh.

*Weddings and campaigns.*

Malcolm answers his phone, "Is this news good, Fred?"

"Layne Osterman will be turned over to the FBI later today. I'm not sure when they will be releasing information about her arrest, but it is going to be a shitshow. You can tell Madison, Mama Girl, Gretchen and the Mitchell's ahead of time. Randy and Peyton already know."

"Understood."

A weird silence takes over.

"Fred."

"Yes, Mr. Mayor."

"Is there something else on your mind?"

"I need a favor."

Malcolm roars in laughter, "The last time someone said that to me, I ended up with a wife."

Fred roars in laughter, "This time I hope I end up with a wife."

Mrs. Mayor places a call to Fred Serpico within two minutes of his ending his call with Mr. Mayor. She starts right in. "I will plan everything. How many people?"

"Four. You and Malcolm. Kittridge and me. It's a surprise by the way."

"Oh, how positively romantic, Fred. And just think, the next president of the United States will be performing the ceremony. When will you be arriving and how long will you be staying?"

"The day after tomorrow and not long enough."

"Three things, Fred. What is Kitt's favorite flower and color and what song is special to you two?"

"Same answer for both flower and color, lavender and sage. *In My Life* by the Beatles."

"See you in two days. Bring a suit, black is best, and don't forget your bride!" Gretchen races to the campaign offices, "Stop what you're doing," she yells to Peyton and Randy. "Grab a paper and pen and follow me." By the time they reach the living room, they have picked up a stray. "Malcolm, don't worry, you won't have a thing to do until the big day."

"Yo, I was at your big day. Was it a misfire?"

"Nope. Fred Serpico is bringing his lovely fiancée to Lewisburg, Pennsylvania, for a surprise wedding right here in this living room. We have lots of things to do, and we have today and tomorrow to do it. Randy, everything in this room, except for the leather couch, needs to be moved out. Call Stephanie Braun and get her moving crew here today. Then call Sweeps, talk to Mavis, and tell her the mayor needs a cleaning crew here two hours ago. The living room and apartment 707 need top to bottom service. If the cleaning crew gets here before the living room is emptied, have them start with the apartment. Peyton, call Right Away Rentals and tell him the mayor needs two round tables for two, ivory linens and ivory lace overlays, two gold standing ice buckets, a black arbor at least 8' tall, twelve 4' black urns, and two 6' black candelabras delivered by no later than 10 AM tomorrow." Gretchen evil-eyes Randy, "Why are you still here? Make your calls. Chop. Chop."

Randy shakes his head as he walks past Malcolm, "I know what I'd like to chop, chop."

Malcolm growls, then laughs, then sprints away with Randy and Peyton.

Gretchen hunts her husband and waits for him to finish his call. While she waits, she receives and answers three texts. When her husband hangs up his phone, she scoots to him, and straddles his lap.

"Don't have time for this, Woman," he smiles wide.

"Do you have time to make a phone call?"

"Fred and Kitt related?"

"Yes. I know I said that—"

"What do you need?"

"Music. Would you call your friend at the School of Music at Bucknell University and see if the—"

"String quartet we had at our wedding is available?"

"Fred and Kitt's song is *In My Life* by The Beatles. The wedding is at 8 PM on Thursday. I want the musicians here no later than six." Gretchen kisses her man, "Plan on a shower later."

The Compound
Fred answers the call from Gretchen, "Hello, Mrs. Mayor."

"Is Kitt with you?"

"Right here, say hello, Kittridge."

"Hi, Gretchen."

Fred listens for a minute, "Hang on. I'll ask. Hey, Kittridge, can we get away for a couple days?"

"Yes! Where are we going, how long are we staying, and do I need something dressy?"

Fred hands the phone to Kitt, "Here, you discuss this with Gretchen, then give me the phone. I need to ask her something about the campaign."

"Gretchen! Yes. Yes. When. When?"

"Malcolm has this dinner thing this Thursday evening. We'd love you and Fred to come with. Malcolm mentioned that Fred sounded really tired the last time he talked to him and suggested that we invite you two down for a few days. I expect you might like a getaway since Fred's been on the road for weeks. Aside from the dinner thing, you two could just hole up in one of the apartments and reconnect or whatever. And you can meet DelRae, that's reason enough to come."

"Good Lord, Fred said your word mashing is legendary, but I don't think I've ever heard one," Kitt says on a laugh. "This sounds wonderful Gretchen, and so thoughtful. I agree with Malcolm, Fred could use a break. Thank you so much. What are you wearing to the dinner?"

"A pretty lavender dress."

"Oh, I love lavender."

"Really?"

"Gosh, I don't think I have anything dressy to fit. I'm four months along, you know."

"Don't worry. There's a boutique at 275. We'll get you something when you arrive. Okay, give me back to Fred for a minute."

Kitt slams the phone against her man's chest. "Move. Move. I've got work to do."

The man in cahoots laughs into the phone. "Nice job, Gretchen."

"She's out of earshot I presume."

"Yeah, she just flung the suitcases onto the bed and she's in the walk-in closet."

"Good. Everything is all set on this end. What time are you arriving?"

"Five."

"Bring her up the back. You're staying in apartment 707, it overlooks Hufnagle. I'll have the place laid out with candles and flowers, and there will be several wedding dresses and things for Kitt to choose from. Oh, Fred, this has been so much fun! Gotta run though, I have a president to elect."

*Keeping secrets.*

Rocco and Joy arrive in DC with Layne Osterman shackled and cuffed at a window seat, requested by the prisoner and granted by Rocco to the dismay of Joy. She eyed her man and whispered, "I'll be getting to the bottom of this allowance on the return flight."

His smile is playful and suggestive, "You are welcome to try, mi amore."

The jet touches down without fanfare, the sound of a steady rain the only witness to the coming events. Within moments, several black SUVs inch across the tarmac and flank the jet, nose to tail and wing to wing. FBI Director Shelby Webber and FICA Director John Maxwell, along with two agents, exit the vehicles and enter the jet. The transfer is underway.

"Layne Osterman, I am FBI Director Shelby Webber. I am placing you under arrest for the assassination of United States Senator Curtis Robert Morgan. Additional charges will be filed against you at a later date. You have the right to remain silent ......."

Rocco and Joy relax in the back of the jet as Layne Osterman is searched, fingerprinted, straightjacketed, and re-shackled. The prisoner doesn't so much as bat an eye as she is handled by a burly buzz cut agent.

Joy head motions John and Shelby as they move to the back of the jet. "You'd need a search party to find a scintilla of emotion in that one."

Shelby nods, "Kind of frightening that Director Maxwell is the emotional one on board."

Joy and Rocco enjoy that little swipe.

John whispers, "Wait until we get home, ma'am, and remind me who the emotional one is."

Joy and Rocco enjoy that, too.

"Can't wait, Caligula."

Joy and Rocco fall out.


Layne Osterman's arrest for the murder of Senator Curtis Robert Morgan from the great state of Georgia knocks all other stories the fuck off of T.V. and print media. RFI and the FBI are hailed as hero organizations. This, despite the hits they're taking for not decimating The Realm their first go round.

Rocco leans back in his office chair enjoying a rarely taken libation with Fred.

"Rocco."

"Si, Fred."

"Let's pencil in another one of these sit downs for when the press finds out we let The Widow roam free."

"Si, Fred."

The Detecting One clears his throat. "Now that Penny and Ted are back at The Compound, and before Leavy et al leave Alaska, I'd like to take a few days away from RFI."

"Si. A good idea. Will the Writing One be accompanying you?"

"She will be leaving with me as my fiancée and returning as my wife—or she will not be returning," Fred's smile stretches across every inch of his face.

Rocco's matches his smile, "Si, a very good idea. Has Kitt knowledge of your plans?"

"Nope."

"Ah, fear not, I am a very good secret keeper." He raises his drink, "Gia used her best feminine wiles to get me to reveal paternity of Turner Rodgers' children. Her efforts, while very pleasurable, were to no avail. I will keep your secrets safe and enjoy my woman's attempts to unseal them."

Fred raises his glass and is quickly brought around, "Wait. You know who fathered the senator's kids."

"Si. And it is quite the secret."

Fred gets up from his chair.

"Where are you going?"

"I've got a wedding to pack for."

*Holy fuck.*

Felicity Ferraro enters her home, pulls a deep breath, and begins her trek upstairs. She removes the hospital scrubs, piece by piece, and drops them along the way. She is naked when she enters her bedroom.

"Welcome home," Mathis says.

Felicity turns and finds her man sitting on the club chair, his feet extended on the ottoman in front. "I was hoping you'd be waiting in the shower or the bed," she smiles as she makes her way to him.

"Wasn't sure when you'd arrive. Love the hair, by the way."

"Love the beach duds." Felicity straddles Mathis and wiggles suggestively.

He moves his legs from the ottoman, lifts her, kisses her, and takes her to the shower where he ravages and devours her. He brings his boneless woman back to the bedroom, "When you're able to stand, get dressed in beachwear. We're leaving in minutes."

"Tell me about the kids."

"They are eagerly awaiting Mommy. Tell me about the Fiancettis."

"They are gloating."

"They're entitled. They are fierce adversaries."

"We'll see how fierce they are when we make our next move."

"Speaking of next moves, I have one, so go get dressed."

Felicity returns to the bedroom wearing an ankle-length, floral gauze dress, wedge-heeled sandals, and broad-brimmed straw hat. She strikes a model's pose, "Well?"

"You wear it well, but not for long." Mathis walks to her, pulls her in for a crushingly passionate kiss, and hands her a note. "Put this into the safe."

Felicity reads it: "She didn't betray me," she laughs, "I just love this—and you, Mathis."

Long after a slow crawl through DC traffic, toward the Chevy Chase residence of Felicity Ferraro, Mike backs the SUV into a grove of trees. He and Ted get out and split up. Ted moves to the side of the house where he'll have a view of the road and the driveway. Mike moves as high onto a hill behind The Widow's house as is possible. He trains his binoculars into the master bedroom. "Holy fuck," he says. He reaches into his pocket for his cell and is knocked unconscious from behind.

## A bride. A groom.
## A Neapolitan crust Prosciutto and Fig pizza.

Rocco places back to back calls to Mike and Ted while he heads to the Computer Center. He locks the door behind him. "Mi amore, trace Michael's and Ted's cells. It is of urgency."

Joy's fingers fly. "They are in Chevy Chase, Maryland. What's going on?"

"They haven't reported in this morning. John is waiting for advisement, please call him."

"John, I have them on satellite images. Mike's behind the Ferraro house on a hill. There's a vehicle on the east side of the house, Ted's in it."

"I'm just pulling in, Joy. Stay on the line ...... Ted's been shot, he's alive and moaning, get two ambulances here. I'm going to find Mike ....... Shit, Joy, he's unconscious and freezing cold, but he's alive. Not sure if I should move him ....... I'm going to cover him and go back to Ted. I need to check his vitals."

"Gia, stay on with John. I'm going to pack and head to the States."

Fred approaches the Land Rover with a concerned look. "What are you doing with an overnight bag, Rocco?"

"I'm coming with you, Fred."

"No. You. Are. Not."

Rocco laughs, "The jet will be dropping you and Kitt in Lewisburg and taking me to DC. That is acceptable, si?"

"Come on."

The ride to the airport and flight to Pennsylvania is quiet. Rocco spends most of his time texting and moving about.

"What's up with Rocco?" Kitt asks.

"No clue. I'm sure there's a lot of shit hitting the fan in DC. Or, in Rocco speak, there's lots of feces flinging and finding whirling devices."

"Si, that is right. We will land in ten minutes. I have a meeting within the hour so I bid goodbyes now."

Fred smiles, "Efficient to a fault."

"Si. Now get out."

"Can we wait until the plane lands?"

"If you must."

## 275

Fred calls Gretchen. "We are at the airport and should be to your place within the hour."

"Put Kitt on."

"She wants to talk to you."

"Hello, Gretchen."

"There's a boutique at 275 called Retro. Have Fred drop you there. And let Fred know there's a snafu with the privacy elevator. It's currently being worked on, so he'll have to use the back entrance. If he needs help schlepping, have him call Randy, he's in the campaign office. And tell Fred your apartment is 707. See you soon!"

Gretchen is over the moon when she sees how wonderfully sweet Kitt looks in the dress she chose for the faux evening out. She goes in for a baby bump rub. "I absolutely hated it when people did this to me, but I just can't help myself."

Kitt smiles then laughs, "I don't mind."

Gretchen steps back, "Turn around, now back. I do declare, Ms. Mahoney, you are with a female baby."

"That's what Fred thinks, but why do you think it's a girl?"

"Nelly in the belly. Jack in the back. That wives tale is based on where your earliest weight gain is, belly for Nelly, back for Jack. Any ounces you've gained are all in the front, that means you're having a girl. Come on, let's find a few accessories to go with that beautiful dress."

"When we're finished, do you want to grab lunch? I'm famished."

"Good, I have a spread already set at the penthouse. We'll just drop off your loot at your apartment, and then eat."

Fred is alerted to the women moving toward 707 when he hears Gretchen say, "Drop your things and meet me upstairs."

Kitt enters the apartment on a giggle, then loses her breath. Fred is standing across the room dressed in a black tux. He walks to her, then takes a knee, "Kittridge, I think it is high time that you become my wife. I suspect you might want our families and friends to be here, but—"

The teary woman cuts him off, "Fred Chester Serpico, I only need you."

Fred stands and takes his woman's face in his hands, "It is 6:15 PM. Our wedding ceremony is at 8 PM. Sharp. I do not want to wait one minute longer than that to be your husband. Gretchen has everything you could ever need or want all set for you in the bedroom. Choose your gown and your shoes or come naked and barefoot. But do not keep me waiting one minute past eight."

Fred brands Kitt with a kiss and leaves.

The groom-to-be knocks on the mayor's door.

"Damn, Fred. You clean up good. You're going to put me to shame."

"Doubt it. Care to show me the wedding venue?"

"Sorry, Fred. I've been banished from the front quarters. I haven't seen my kitchen in two days. Hang on." Malcolm answers his cell, "Woman? Are you within hearing distance?"

"Nope, I have your office bugged. Please bring the groom to the living room."

"Woman, you might want to be sitting. Fred is looking right fine."

"Bring him!"

There are dueling gasps. Hers over the likes of Fred. Theirs over the transformation of the living room. "It's like we landed on a magical planet," Malcolm opines.

"I know. I haven't a clue how to move, or if I should."

Malcolm pulls his wife near, "You did real good, Gretchen." Mr. and Mrs. Price watch quietly as Fred inches about.

"Kittridge is going to love this. Tell me what I'm seeing here, Gretchen."

"The flowers are predominantly lavender and sage with ivory Astrantia, lace Asclepias, wedding kale, and cream carnations. The placement of the urns form the aisle, and between the candelabras is where you will exchange your vows. To the right of the windows is a video camera. Randy has set it so you can record the event or he can livestream it so everyone at The Compound can watch. To the left of the windows will be where you and Kitt and Malcolm and I will dine. Peyton handled the catering of your selection and will serve the requested Neapolitan crust Prosciutto and Fig pizza. In the corner by the elevator is where the string quartet will be. They are inhouse and waiting for our call. Now, if you will excuse me, I have some personal primping to do. I have Kitt's bouquet and will give it to her at precisely 8:00 PM. Malcolm, I expect you and Fred at those candelabras by 7:45."

"Yes, ma'am."

Fred slaps Malcolm on the shoulder. "That woman of yours is First Lady material."

"Agreed."

*Kittridge Mahoney*

*&*

*Fred Serpico*

*request the honor of your presence*

*as they exchange vows of marriage.*


Gretchen knocks on 707 at 7:07. Kitt answers the door in tears.

"Oh no. No. No. What's wrong?"

"Nothing. Everything is perfect. Too perfect to be kept from everyone."

"Oh, Kitt. We can handle this. Randy set a video camera to record the ceremony, and he set a live feed to The Compound if you want to use it."

The waterworks turn to a trickle. The bride tilts her head in thought, "No to the live feed, and thank you to the video. I really want this to be about Fred and me. Just knowing everyone can see it later settles the matter." Kitt turns toward the bedroom, then turns back. "Oh, Gretchen, I didn't even mention how beautiful you look. The lavender is absolutely perfect on you, and the dress compliments the one I chose."

Gretchen squeals in delight and claps her hands, "I just knew you were going to choose the ivory lace. Come, let's get you dressed."

Kitt slips off her robe and Gretchen gets to work. She lifts the form fitting, sweetheart sheath over Kitt's head, then adds the all lace, long-sleeved, crew-neck overlay. She buttons the five crystals at the back of the neck, "How are you going to wear your hair?"

"In a deconstructed updo with a few stray ringlets. Fred loves my hair that way."

"Perfect. The buttons in back are very pretty and should be seen, and they match these." Gretchen hands her wedding earrings to Kitt. "If you would like to wear them, they will handle the old and the borrowed. My mother wore them on her wedding day, and I on mine."

"They are beautiful, Gretchen. I'd be so pleased to wear them."

"The new is your wedding dress and the blue is in this box."

Kitt million-watts her friend when she finds a sweet blue and ivory lace garter. "How did you know I'd choose the ivory gown?"

"I may not be a spy, Kitt, buy I have certain skills."

Gretchen calls Malcolm. "We are ready. Please instruct the music to begin when they see me. Thank you." Gretchen goes to the refrigerator and removes a box; from it she lifts Kitt's bouquet.

"Oh, Gretchen, it is perfectly lovely. Lavender and sage, carnations and Astrantia. I am unfamiliar with the other flowers, but they are beautiful."

"Lace Asclepias and ivory wedding kale. They are what I call refined wildflowers. They reminded me of you, you're refined, but you have an unbridled nature."

Kitt laughs, "I think that is the nicest way anyone's ever described me."

"Let's go, so I can describe you as Mrs. Fred Serpico." When Gretchen turns to make her entrance to the living room the beautiful strings of *In My Life* lift from the quartet. Gretchen finds Kitt's eyes before she begins her walk. "Watch the violinist, when she nods, start the walk to your man."

Fred's breath is stolen when Kitt appears at the end of the aisle. She pauses a moment before her walk. Her eyes never leave Fred's. At the end of the aisle, she hands Gretchen her bouquet and places her hand into Fred's outstretched one.

"Words are going to fail me, Kittridge. My feelings are controlling this moment."

Silence fills the space. Gretchen breaks it, "Mr. Mayor, I believe you have words to say."

"I am honored to officiate at this union and delighted to witness the promises made by two wonderful people and cherished friends.

Kittridge Mahoney and Fred Serpico, do you enter into marriage with the intensions to love and support one another?"

"We do."

"Do you promise to stand with one another and offer yourselves to no other throughout all the days that follow?"

"We do."

Malcolm steps back.

Fred steps to his bride. "Kittridge, a very long time ago you said that you fell in love with me on our faux date. I told you that it took me until our faux, faux date before I fell for you. That was a lie. I fell in love with you the moment I laid eyes on you. I surrendered my heart to you the day we stood at the stone arch on Farmington Road. I offered you my life when we stood with our boy at the shore of Laurel Falls. With you by my side, Kittridge, I will want for nothing and have everything." He slips a simple band onto her finger and places a kiss upon it.

Gretchen steps forward and hands Kitt a ring, "A surprise wedding does not allow time for all things. I took the liberty of sharing news of your nuptials with my father. He brought this ring by this morning for you to give to Fred. It may not fit, but it is placeholder and a gift from Granger should you two decide to keep it." She turns to the groom, "My father was given this ring the day he married my mother. He wore it for many years and said it holds a place of importance in his heart. Granger considers you more than a friend, Fred. He thinks of you as a son. He asked me to express that to you." Gretchen turns to leave the makeshift altar, then turns back, "I guess this makes us siblings, Fred."

He laughs big, "You're a pisser, Gretchen."

Kitt takes her intended's hand. "Fred. The love you give me is complete and uncomplicated. I never have to wonder about us." She tears a bit. He gently pads away those that slip, and whispers, "I will always choose you." She offers the smile that captured his heart the day they met. "I know ……. Fred, the surety of who we are as a couple has steadied me through some hard times. I am more deeply in love you, and with us, than I have ever been, and I am quite ready to promise the rest of my days to you. With you by my side, Fred, I will want for nothing and have everything." She slips the perfect fitting band onto his finger and places a kiss upon it.

Malcolm steps forward. "Kittridge and Fred, you have expressed your intentions and made your promises. Without further pause, and with great pride, I say these words for the first time, by the power vested in me as Mayor of the Borough of Lewisburg in the Commonwealth of Pennsylvania, I am delighted to pronounce you husband and wife. You may…"

*For things aren't
what they seem.*


Randy waits until dinner and dancing is done, then approaches Malcolm, "I need a minute." The men move to the entertainment room. "Annie Mahoney-Maxwell has been trying to get in touch with Kitt and Fred. She reached out to me for help. Mike Monopoli and Ted Brothers were attacked and left for dead outside the home of Felicity Ferraro. Mike has a concussion, and Ted took a bullet to an arm and lost a lot of blood. Both men are in the hospital in Chevy Chase, Maryland. Rocco and John Maxwell are with them and plan on flying them home on the same flight with Fred and Kitt in two days. My question is what should we do about Annie? She said she knows they are at some dinner with you and Gretchen, but she hopes to get a call from them sometime tonight."

"She will. The newlyweds are enjoying some alone time in the penthouse. When they head to their apartment, I'll tell them what's going on. Thank you and Peyton for all your help."

Chevy Chase
John leaves the hospital once Mike regains consciousness and Ted is out of surgery. He

heads directly to The Widow's home, goes around to the back to begin picking the lock, and finds he doesn't need to. He enters the house, gun in hand. He's familiar with the place from his earlier B&E trip and heads directly to the bedroom, smirks when he finds the bed empty, but recently used, "A little debauchery for the road?" He scans the room and finds the safe wide open. He pulls a slip of paper from inside and reads: "She didn't betray me." John backtracks through the house, gets into his SUV, and calls Rocco. "First, how are Mike and Ted?"

"Wounded, but able to travel the day after tomorrow. Anything at the house?"

"A note. I'm assuming you'll know it's meaning."

"Proceed."

"She didn't betray me."

"Damn him! Mathis Reynolds orchestrated everything."

"Explain."

"When we told The Widow we were sending her back to DC, she said she couldn't go back, but presented no real objection. She expressed amusement over Thorndyke's suicide and that Gang members and Turner Rodgers placed calls to Thorndyke incriminating themselves. When she learned Mathis Reynolds made a similar call, she showed no emotion."

"Did she ask if the immunity issue was settled?"

"No."

"Did she mention her children?"

"No. She acted unhinged. She started antagonizing Gia in Irish slang. Accused her of being a chancer by allowing the enemy within the fortress." Rocco pauses, "Her final words were in Gaelic, but Gia translated them."

"Explain."

"For things aren't what they seem."

"For fucks sake. She played us, they played us. Mathis Reynolds was no threat to the Ferraro children."

"No, but he is a threat to The Compound. The Widow knows far too much about us."

## *Did I miss anything?*

The RFI jet lands in Nova Scotia with five onboard: Mr. Fiancetti, Mr. and Mrs. Serpico, a concussed and stitched Mike Monopoli, and a stitched and slung Ted Brothers. No mention of Fred and Kitt's nuptials were made until Ted notices Fred's wedding band.

"Fred Serpico, did you take yourself a wife?"

Fred smiles as wide as humanly possible, "Yes, I did Theodore."

"I'll be damned. Wake up Mike, we have newlyweds onboard."

A groggy Mike turns heavy eyes toward Fred and Kitt, who are holding up their wedding-banded hands so Mike can see their rings. He closes his eyes and groans, "Damned concussion. Now I'm seeing things."

The wedding rings are completely overlooked by the occupants of The Compound, as everyone's attention is laser focused on the injured men. Steve, Penny, and Annie escort them to the Medical Center where Maura and the two FBI medically trained agents await their arrival.

Fred and Kitt accompany Rocco to the office for a complete update on what happened in Chevy Chase.

"Mike and Ted were dispatched to The Widow's house to see if she returned after her discharge from the hospital. Ted was near their vehicle on the side of the house nearest the driveway. He heard a step behind him, turned, and was shot. The bullet was a through and through wound to his arm. He said he was going to yell out to Mike, but he took a foot to the face to silence him. Mike said he didn't hear a thing, but was focused on getting into place on the hill. When he set himself and looked into the master bedroom, he saw The Widow and The Body in bed. He reached for his phone, and the next thing he knew he was waking up in an ambulance."

"Mathis and Felicity were in on this," Fred concludes.

"Si. They pulled one over on us."

"Let me run this, Rocco, and see if we end up at the same place."

"Si."

"The Widow knew she was being surveilled by Mike. She dropped a note that read: **I know everything. I want full immunity.** She was given the opportunity to work with the FBI, but John suggested she work with RFI because we are better equipped to find her kids. She came to The Compound, flipped on everyone in

The Realm, including Mathis Reynolds—but we already knew he was The Body, so her information about him was irrelevant. We went into her place, without warrant for search and seizure, because we needed to keep her kidnapping a secret from The Body. We got files, thumb drives, and ledgers to support what she told us, but RFI and the FBI can't use any of that stuff. The FBI gave her full immunity, and we gave her our assurances that we wouldn't move on the DC criminals until her children were found. Meanwhile, Carter Thorndyke thought Felicity Ferraro was kidnapped and knew he'd be blamed, so he freaked and killed himself. We looked at that event as an opportunity to get The Widow back to DC so The Body would think she'd been kidnapped by Thorndyke and wouldn't suspect we had her and she flipped on him. The night she was discharged from the hospital, Mathis Reynolds was in her home awaiting her return. After fucking up our men, they disappeared into the night. The Widow gets her kids and The Body gets his woman. Did I miss anything?"

"No, Detecting One."

Fred gets up, and offers his hand to his bride. She snuggles under his arm and whispers, "I'm glad I know how to shoot shit."

# Snowfall Prison

In the wee hours, Hannah Leavy is escorted out of Cabin 5. It's the first time she asks where she is, "Am I in Alaska?"

"Yes. This area is inside Kenai National Wildlife Refuge."

"And that's where?"

"Close enough to Anchorage, Miss."

"Travel time?"

"Airport to airport about eight hours. Total trip, closer to twelve."

"So I'll see him, them, sometime today?"

"Leavy, you will see who you want to see or no one at all."

"Can I have a pill?"

The doctor checks his watch, "No."

"Before the flight?"

"Yes."

# HOME

It is dark when the jet touches down in Halifax. The travelers get into a Land Rover and make a silent trip to The Compound. When they arrive they are met by Rocco Fiancetti, who makes no move toward the woman whose head is slung low. "You are home, Leavy."

Weinstock supports her weight when she pushes near, "Is the medical suite ready?"

"Si. The entire space is for Leavy and your team."

After the doctor and his patient leave, Rocco Fiancetti pulls his friend, Wooly Jones, in for a hug. "Thanks are inadequate."

"And unnecessary."

"Come, let me show you to your place."

"Coordinates will be fine."

"Si. Head to the river, follow south a half mile, and the cottage is a couple thousand yards into the woods. Head back this way in the morning. There's something I could use your help with."

"I'm staying awhile?"

"Si." Before Rocco can leave, he is approached by a steaming Annie. "Piccolo, I'm sensing bigilo anger."

"Si. Fair warning, Mr. Fiancetti, Piccolo is pissed." Annie's attention is averted by the slam of a screen door and the approach of Fred and Kitt. She shoots them a warning, "Don't get involved. As for you Mr. Fiancetti, I have a simple question, and I'd appreciate an explanation that is forthright and acceptable to me, or this conversation intends to be a lengthy one."

"Si, but of course."

"When you left the other morning, you already knew Mike and Ted were injured," she huffs.

"Si."

"Why didn't you take Penny and me with you?" she puffs.

Rocco begins to speak.

Fred cuts him off. "He didn't want you on the plane with your mother and me."

"Why not?"

Fred and Kitt raise their left hands showing off their wedding rings.

"Married? Mike said you were married. I thought he had permanent brain damage." She turns on her heels and marches away.

"Not the reaction I expected," Fred grumbles.

"Isn't it?" Kitt laughs.

# Leavy

Weeks pass with Leavy remaining close to the medical suite. If she goes out, it is to the boat dock, where she sits quietly for hours. Today, she has agreed to go for a walk along Roseway River with Candace Hayes. Residents of The Compound were sent a communication that no one is allowed outside while Leavy moves about. Every few steps or so, the young woman stops—the first few times it is to look over her shoulder and to scan her surroundings—the next many times it is to lift her face to the sun. After a good bit of walking, Leavy stops and leans against a large river rock. "Candace, if you were to follow the path behind me, you'd end up at the cottage I used to share with Manuel."

"Yes."

"You knew that?"

"I did."

"Have you been to the cottage?"

"My husband asked me to meet him there last week."

"Husband?"

"Gregory. Dr. Weinstock."

"You're married? To him?"

"I am. Three months today, in fact."

Leavy smiles. "Three months. What was your wedding date?"

"December 5th."

Leavy gets up and looks beyond Candace in the direction of a cabin she can't see, but knows is there, "Is today March 5th?"

"Yes."

"Today is Manuel's birthday."

"Yes."

"He told you?"

"No, I saw it on his medical chart."

"You took care of him … after the shooting?"

"Yes."

"He must have been hurt very badly for the FBI to send a whole team for him."

"Yes. Mr. Xavier is very lucky to be seeing another birthday."

Leavy scoffs. "I guess we are both very lucky to have survived the Reynolds brothers."

# Manuel

The birthday boy dumps his drink into the sink, walks past Weinstock, and heads outside.

"Don't even think about trying to find Leavy," Weinstock says from the door of the cottage. "I don't feel like chasing you or tackling you, but make no mistake, I will do both."

"She's bonding with you and pushing me aside."

"Yes. The goal is for her to move beyond me. I want you to be an option for her, Manuel. At the moment, you are not." Weinstock walks to the emotionally wounded man and puts his hand on his shoulder. "You need to come to terms with something. Leavy isn't the woman you last held in your arms. She may never return to you in that way. Because of the love you feel for her, Manuel, you need to shoulder that burden, and let her become who she is going to be, whether that is with you or without you."

Weinstock waits as Manuel works through what he just said. "Manuel, I saw you spit in the face of death. I saw you move physical boulders aside. I saw you struggle for a foothold, then find your stride. I paid witness to your physical pain, and now, I am party to a whole new round of injury and suffering—the kind that may have no healing. I know what you want and what you need. That's not what you get right now. The only thing you get is the gift of knowing Leavy is alive and breathing as a free woman. That's it. Accept it. And learn to deal with it, Manuel."

"Maybe if I see her, or talk to her, or hold her, she'll come back."

"If you force her to do any of those things, you will never have her in your life. As hard as it is, you need to be the one who doesn't force her, the one who waits for her. You need to be the anti-Eli."

# The Campaign

## April

After Kitt and Fred's wedding, the living room at 275 remained free of furniture. Gretchen converted the space to an executive suite for the senior staff of the Malcolm Price for President campaign. Madison Morgan moved into one of the apartments at 275 for the duration. She and Mama Girl work primarily in the executive suite, as will Granger and Faye when they return from "Honeymoon Interruptus" as Randy refers to their belated trip of wedded bliss.

## May

The frenzy over which government officials were part of The Realm and the wafting stench of corruption permeating out of DC caused Gretchen to abandon the idea of Malcolm participating in Democratic and/or Republican primary debates. She explained her thoughts during a mandatory all-staff meeting at 275. "Our candidate is not stepping foot on a sullied stage with anyone! Turner Rodgers is barely holding on, though he seems determined to ride his slippery slope to the gutter. The Republican Party won't cut their losses until he bails or finds his ass in jail, which is all the better for us. If the GOP has a candidate in the wings who can legitimately take on Morrisey or Price, they haven't so much as hinted at it."

Madison offers her assessment, "As for Jim Morrisey, the congressman from the 1st District of Missouri is taking his fair share of heat for being part of the DC sewer, deservedly or not. Though he's a Democrat, most of his economic and some of his social policies are more closely aligned with the Republicans, which might appeal to voters who decide to bail on Turner Rodgers."

"On that point, Madison, according to a Missouri poll conducted two days ago, in a head to head general election between Price and Morrisey, Democrats overwhelmingly support Price, while Republicans favor Morrisey, though not by a significant margin. This bodes well for Malcolm." Gretchen begins cooing to DelRae who's decided to weigh in with a squirm and a squeal. Campaign manager-mom lifts her little one from her playmat and finishes the meeting. "Everyone back to whatever you were doing or were supposed to be doing. Meet back here one month from today. Those of you who have weekly scheduled meetings, don't be late, and bring good reports."

## June

"Mayor Price will be heading to the following states for rallies and sit down interviews. Democratic safe states: Washington, and Oregon. Democratic likely and leaning states: Colorado, New Mexico, and Nevada. Toss up states: Arizona, Wisconsin, and Michigan. Republican safe states: Missouri. Republican likely and leaning states: Texas, Ohio, Georgia, and North Carolina. If the candidate is expecting information, input, or itinerary plans, provide them. Deadline is two days prior. A bit of news, so listen up, folks, our campaign has it on very good authority that Turner Rodgers will be out of the race soon." Gretchen happily waits through a robust round of hoots and hollers. "Okay. Okay. Settle, please. GOP voters are already choosing between Morrisey and Price in three-way polling. Most are moving toward Morrisey, but a larger number of Democrats are moving away from Morrisey toward Price."

Madison offers insight into the candidate from Missouri. "Morrisey is walking a fine line. He's courting conservatives and hoping he doesn't alienate liberals and progressives. At some point the voters are going to push him to one side of the line or the other. Our candidate will stay in his lane. He is fiscally responsible, socially liberal, and unwavering in his commitment to environmental issues, healthcare for all, fair and balanced immigration policies, and preserving and strengthening Medicare and Medicaid. That is this campaign's message. Those of you who are authorized to speak on behalf of this campaign, learn it and repeat it. Often."

"Okay, some campaign updates. Madison Morgan, Peyton Wells, and Randy Parker will be accompanying Malcom on his trips. They will rotate in and out as needs present themselves. Security will be provided by RFI on a rotating basis. Steve Phelps, Ted Brothers, and Penny Meehan are slated for the first group. That's it. Everyone back to whatever you were doing or were supposed to be doing. Meet back here one month from today. Those of you who have weekly scheduled meetings, don't be late, and bring good reports."

## July

"Our 'No Mudslinging Campaign' is working to our advantage. Every sit down interview Malcolm has had, the interviewer pressed him on what he thinks about Morrisey's opinion pieces from law school defending men's equal rights in abortion decisions, even in the case of rape and incest, his opposition to same sex marriage, and his support of Don't Ask Don't Tell being reinstituted. Our candidate reminds the interviewer that Morrisey has gone on record recanting those opinions. Then he states his own unwavering position on a women's right to choose and his belief that all men and women are created equal and are entitled to equal rights under Constitutional law and the laws of decency and morality. Polls suggest the repetition of these questions are moving Democratic voters away from Morrisey's conservative views, even if the voters aren't falling in lockstep with our Independent candidate, they sure are listening to his positions and agreeing with them. I believe Mr. Malcolm Price is destined to be our next president." She reels her team in after some well-deserved frivolity. "Okay, okay. That's the good news. The troubling thing for our campaign is that Rodgers is quite busy slinging mud at Curtis Morgan and Bertha King Price. He knows he doesn't stand a chance in November, but he wants his pound of flesh against the son of the man who would have beaten him at the polls. Our candidate is holding his own when the tender spot of his father is pushed, but there's some heat under his collar over this. He's been away a long time and is anxious to get back to 275. I expect to be apprised at the first sign that Mayor Price is stepping too close to our mandated line, or that Morrisey is getting in on the mudslinging on Curtis Morgan, Bertha King Price, or on Sage Finley. Everyone back to whatever you were doing or were supposed to be doing. Meet back here one month from today. Those of you who have weekly scheduled meetings, don't be late, and bring good reports."

## August

The traveling road show is back in Lewisburg. Before heading to the monthly meeting, the husband asks for some private time with his wife. He pulls her into his embrace. "Well, well, Mr. Price, it seems last night's debauchery has not satisfied your wanting."

"Satisfied me just fine, but I need to press in for a bit."

Gretchen takes her man's face in her hands, "Is something wrong?"

"Just need you, Woman."

"The attacks on Curtis and Bertha, they are getting to you."

"My father is gone. The attacks can't hurt him. They aren't even about him. They are about Madison. The GOP candidate knows there is a winning ticket in the making."

Gretchen ponders. Gretchen reacts. "You want Madison as your vice-presidential running mate. Inspired."

"Turner has analyzed Madison and me on the campaign trail. He sees what I see."

"A winning ticket. What about Madison? Does she know where your thoughts are taking you?"

"She suspects. And I think she would do it."

"But?"

"The assassination." Malcolm walks away from his wife, finds a spot against the wall and leans in. "My announcement to run for president in the Cathedral that morning was fueled by anger and hubris. I was inches from my assassinated father, and I never considered that I put a target on my back, and yours, and Madison's, and Mama Girl's."

She joins him, leans into him. "Malcolm, a calling to greatness shouldn't be encumbered. Madison shouldn't be protected from her calling. If you want her by your side, tell her. Don't rob either of you the opportunity to choose." Gretchen leaves her husband to his reflection. "Work this through, and meet me in the shower in ten minutes. If you are late, Mr. Mayor, I'm starting without you."

Malcolm pushes off the wall and chases his wife, "Decision made. Now for a little gentling."

Gretchen is all smiles when she enters the Campaign office. Her smile widens when she answers a call from Fred Serpico. "What a delightful surprise!"

"You already know?"

"Know what?"

"Kittridge had our baby girl. She said to call you immediately and accuse you of being a witch. I happily accepted the directive."

"Oh, Fred. How are Kitt and the baby ...... ooooo, do you have a name?"

"They are wonderful. And the baby's name is Laurel Anne Serpico."

Gretchen catches on, "Ohhhh, how sweet. You named her after Laurel Falls. It's lovely that the two of you found a most beautiful way to bring your home to The Compound."

## September

Turner Rodgers is out of the race. For the first time in American political history, a Democrat and an Independent will be on the general election presidential ballot without a member of the GOP. If Malcolm Price is elected, he will be the second Independent to take the Oath of Office, the first being George Washington.

## October

Malcolm and the new woman in his life are campaigning across the country. The original ticket of father and son is now the ticket of son and stepmother. Chants of Malcolm and Morgan raise high from sea to shining sea.

## November

Daily polls predict Malcolm Price, former NBA point guard, former correctional officer, son of the late Curtis Robert Morgan and Bertha King Price, stepson of Madison Carlisle Morgan, mayor of Lewisburg, Pennsylvania, husband of Gretchen Delaney Mitchell, and father of

DelRae Finley Price is going to be the 46th President of the United States of America.

# Election Night

275 Market Street, Lewisburg, Pennsylvania, is floor to rafter and wall to wall full of friends and family. Every seventh floor apartment is occupied by RFI members, and every room on the eighth floor is in celebration. The President-elect and next First Lady of the United States are sharing a dance in the living room. Baby Girl is in the arms of Mama Girl. The Vice President-elect is in quiet reflection with Granger and Faye Mitchell. The Kid and The Justice are moving about streaming live shots to friends and family who could not be at the festivities.

Manuel is spending time with Leavy at the medical suite watching the festivities with Dr. and Mrs. Weinstock, who are back at The Compound for an employment interview. Rocco and Joy are in the great room listening to the hoots and hollers from the lower level. They are raising their glasses in quiet toast to the new president when a voice comes from behind them.

"Mrs. Fiancetti. Please come with me.
Mr. Fiancetti, if you move, you die."

When the echo of gunfire subsides, and Mathis Reynolds drives from the Fiancetti fortress with the preeminent cyber huntress formerly known as DOA, Manuel Xavier places a frantic call to Fred Serpico.

"Joy is gone!!!!!"

The End

More to come … someday …

*Alva*

# ALVA

## THE BODY

--- PULLING THREADS ---

A RFI Investigation

SHERYLL O'BRIEN

# ABOUT THE AUTHOR

She is not dead.

Sheryll O'Brien crafts characters without constraints. She tells them who they are, then let's them show her better versions of themselves. She gives them life and they live it beyond her wildest dreams.

Sheryll is a lifelong resident of Worcester, Massachusetts, where she is wife to the most supportive husband ever, and mother of two adult daughters, one who refuses to leave her home and the other who refuses to tell her where she lives. Of most significance, she is MammyGrams to the sweetest six-year-old, Hadley.

Sheryll worked several years in the fundraising community of Worcester County, writing grants for non-profit organizations. She began writing for her own pleasure after surviving brain surgery and breast cancer. Happily, for her fanbase of family and friends-—she is not dead.

If you have enjoyed reading my book, I would very much appreciate you taking a few minutes to write a review and post that review on amazon.com and goodreads.com.

The opinion of readers can help prospective readers make a purchasing decision.

To learn more, please visit my website, www.pullingthreadsnovella.com subscribe to my blog for updates on future projects.

I would absolutely love to hear from my readers, you can email me at,

pullingthreadsnovella@gmail.com